BLOOD MOON

Blood Moon
(Blood Rights, Book Three)

K. B. Thorne

To the melodramatic, goth teens that my husband (who wrote the bit that started this book) and I were as teens. We let you just bleed your angst all over this.

CHAPTER ONE

Call it what you want.

It was that untamable, undeniable, inescapable hunger I had, and it grew with every passing hour. Some might compare it to the first time you heard the roar of a Camaro—the only way it was meant to be heard, with eight cylinders and nothing holding it back from ripping itself right out of the car. Others might think of it as that unfed monster that dwells in your gut after the first time you've flown, that taste of the sky and the edge of the earth that leaves you wanting more and more. *Voracious.* That's it. The hunger I had was voracious, and it grew worse by the day.

Little did I know exactly what that meant for me.

I suppose I had always been restless. I was the kid who couldn't sit still. I turned into the teenager who chased things in cyberspace when I wasn't earning speeding tickets or getting shot down by girls far out of my league. When my job offered the chance for a transfer up North, I packed up my Southern roots and replanted them in Connecticut, no matter who got left behind.

Despite trying to put a thousand miles between this feeling and me, it was still there. Every day, it seemed to grow a little more. The hunger was a black hole threatening to swallow the galaxy of my life. No matter what I tried, I couldn't seem to find what would fill it. I tried. Believe me, I tried, but the hunger was insatiable.

It was voracious.

The first night when that black hole seemed poised to suck everything into it at last, I woke up with the mother of all hangovers. It was so bad that it had swallowed much of the night before, which had been my goal in the first place. Anything to escape my life's monotony, though it usually didn't work.

I peeled my eyelids apart, but when the bright light assaulted me, I shut them again. After a few moments, I gave it another shot and managed to look around, learning I'd fallen asleep on my sofa. That was unusual. I usually made it to the bed.

Last night careened through my mind in the briefest of flashes. Most of it was the same as always, but there was the occasional intrusion of a woman across the room. She stared with an intensity one didn't usually enjoy without either being fucked senseless or found cut up in the freezer two months later.

Pushing myself up to a seat, I realized the television was playing. In all the brief flashes of memory, I didn't have one of me turning it on. If I'd had my choice, it definitely wouldn't have been the news, which was what was playing.

"Senator Joshua Clancy has issued a statement regarding the disappearance of his daughter, fourteen-year-old Sandra, last January..." I half-listened. I remembered hearing about that a few times. The teenaged daughter of a state senator doesn't disappear without making some headlines. The newscaster continued. *"The Connecticut senator was instrumental in the passing of the Preternatural Rights Act of twenty-ten, also known as Cameron's Law, the controversial legislation making all preternatural creatures legal citizens. It's feared that the disappearance of Miss Clancy is retribution for his role..."*

I started drowning the woman's voice out again, but couldn't help but think that sounded pretty shitty. I mean, I didn't like the idea of grocery shopping with werewolves any better than anyone else, but kidnapping a guy's kid? That just seemed low, if that was the case.

Turning off the television, I dragged myself to the bathroom and tried to brush the cotton out of my mouth. The shower was next, hoping to slough life off. That didn't work, but I got the dirt, sweat, and oil. It was a start, though looking in the mirror afterward, I saw dark shadows under my eyes that were pronounced against my pale complexion. At least they matched my hair. Even so, I looked and felt like hammered shit.

Whatever the hell I had ended up drinking last night, I made a sober promise to never drink it again.

By the time I returned to the living room in a clean pair of jeans and an equally clean black T-shirt, I smelled better but still felt like roadkill. I slumped in front of my shiny custom-built computer and booted it up, waiting through the usual startup routines and typing distractedly through password protection windows. When it was done, I looked at my desktop and saw that it was 8:30. The darkness through the window assured me it was PM and not AM. Damn. My boss was going to be pissed. How had I managed to sleep through the entire day?

I hadn't even managed to open a program before the door to my apartment slammed open and bounced against the wall. The sound ricocheted off the inside of my skull, and I spun to face the intruder.

"D, where the fuck have you been?" My lovely girlfriend Raven screeched in a way appropriate to her nickname. (Her real name was Henrietta Lowenstein, but it was death to anyone who used it. I called her that a lot and remained remarkably alive.) She slammed the door closed with a platform-encased foot. "I've been waiting on your sorry ass for over an hour now!"

Putting her hands on her hips, which I'll grant were part of a decent enough figure, she fixed me with a glare. At least, I thought it was a glare. It could be hard to read her expression under the black lipstick and pale face powder, as well as blue eye shadow that no one had mentioned wasn't supposed to go up to the brow like that.

"For fuck's sake, keep your voice down," I murmured, getting up from my desk and crossing to the couch. Like that would help me escape. "What are you talking about?"

She huffed. "You forgot about me, didn't you?"

I pressed the heels of my hands against my eyes. "Obviously," I said. My brain tried to retreat from the auditory assault, but it didn't get far.

She sat down beside me and smacked me upside the head. "Hey, dickwad! You're ignoring me again!"

"Trying to ignore your bitching when I have a pounding fucking headache is justified." I pried an eye open to glower at her. Normally, the low-cut top would be enough to pull me out of my bad mood, but this pit was too deep to see sunlight. Or boobs, even.

She glared right back. "Don't get an attitude. You are the one who forgot me tonight, after all, so *I* get to be the pissy one."

That part was hard to argue with. "Could you be pissy on mute?"

Cupping her hands around her black-painted lips, she shouted, "No!"

I sunk into the couch cushions and pulled the pillow over my head. "Get out of my apartment, you fucking psycho." I waited until I heard the door shut before looking out. I was relieved.

Normally I didn't aim to be quite such a bastard, but I felt miserable, and her lack of sympathy brought out the big bastard in me.

After a while, I forced myself to my feet. Wandering to my window, I looked out over the city that *truly* never slept.

Maybe it used to be New York, but now that Adelheid, CT, was the hub of preternatural life, the humans took over the day and the fangs took over the night, with the rest somewhere in between.

I wasn't too keen on any of them, but I'd hardly known this place for what it was when I moved here several years ago. By the time Cameron's Law was a done deal, I couldn't afford to go elsewhere, so I just tried to avoid most of the populace.

Leaving the window, I was headed back to my computer when my cell rang, mangling *Moonlight Sonata* in a way that only technology can. I looked at the ID, but answered it anyways.

"D," Geoffrey blared in my ear. "Where the hell are ya, man?! We're all waiting for you. Rave is already down here hittin' the shooters."

"Yeah, she was here and left in a bitchy huff. I think we've broken up again, so I'm not sure anywhere near her is really where I want to be." I didn't owe him an explanation. Fact was, the guy tended to annoy the hell out of me, but my aching head apparently forced me into honesty.

"Oh, come on, D, we're all dying to know if you ever found out who that chick was staring at you last night."

I paused. They had noticed that? I wondered if any of them knew more than I did and could give me some clues; name and phone number would be nice. Hey, I was newly single, right? It was enough to entice me to leave my apartment after all. "I'll be there in a bit." I hung up without saying good-bye, because I didn't need his loud voice in my ear anymore.

Slipping into my heavy boots, I grabbed my wallet and keys and made my way onto the streets. It was a warm summer night, so I didn't need anything else. I drove to the center of town where Phoenix was, wondering if tonight might actually be a night where something new happened.

CHAPTER TWO

With an ugly fluorescent hand stamp of what was supposed to be a phoenix, but just looked like a dead chicken, I walked into Phoenix. It was...the same as it always was: stuffed from wall to wall with people either drinking around the edges or all crammed onto the dance floor, shuffling in the same drug-induced stupor. It wasn't exactly dancing, but it wasn't quite an X-fueled rave either. If one didn't know better, they might think it was a mass breakout of the zom-pocalypse.

Now that was a thought that was gonna fester.

It didn't take long to find my friends, or at least the people I hung out with. With Geoffrey being quite as flaming gay as he was, I could find him like a beacon of light in any crowd. Not that I had a problem with it. It was probably the only interesting thing about him, aside from the way he came to the club every night looking like he'd been beaten with a glitter stick and enjoyed it.

Stuffing my hands in my pockets, I walked up to the table, adopting the look of the anti-socialite trying to be social. Tony was there with a girl under each arm. They were spending most of their attention on each other. Geoffrey was sitting on the lap of some muscle head without much by way of intelligence in his eyes. And then there was Rave, lip-locked with some goofy-looking bastard I didn't recognize.

"Wow, Raven, didn't even take you half an hour," I commented. I don't know why I bothered, but I couldn't seem to help myself.

She pulled herself away to fix me with my third glare of the evening. "Fuck you, D."

I smirked. "You already did, and quite frankly, you could have tried harder."

Tony's two girls separated long enough to give the appropriate 'owned' noise while Raven huffed and puffed and dragged her new boyfriend away.

"Gee, I wonder what set her off." I dropped myself into the now-empty seat.

"You really are an ass, D." This was from Geoffrey, who was only paying half of his attention to me. He laughed. From the glossy look in his eyes, I knew he was high on something, but damned if I cared that much.

Five minutes and already I felt twitchy. Aside from my apparent break-up, there was nothing different about tonight. It all felt the same. It was the same damn stuff every damn day with blinding monotony. The DJ played the same bass-thumping 'music.' The people dancing all danced the same moves, like a badly drawn animation. The pounding came back, and I knew it wasn't my hangover. It was the hunger. It growled again, looking for that magical something I didn't know. I almost got up to leave but instead forced myself to let my eyes roam instead.

They happened on a small cluster of people nearby. I recognized one of them from television: Sadie Stanton, poster girl for preternatural rights. I knew she was a vampire.

"Who invited the fang crowd?" I muttered, turning back to the table and slouching in my seat. Every head turned toward them and then back toward me.

"Watch out, D." This from the girl with Tony I thought was named Liza. "Their hearing is better than your ability to be quiet."

I turned my head back to see the three of them looking

in my direction. All wore dark expressions and one—a thick man who looked Hispanic—took a step toward us, and I felt a gut level fear for my throat. My hand almost went to it, but Stanton put her hand on his arm. She said something I couldn't hear, and he stepped back, but continued to glare at me. I sighed inwardly with relief. They didn't want to do anything to fuck up Cameron's Law and give others a reason to rescind it. My sense of safety returned, and I looked at my 'crew' again.

"What do you have against them anyways?" Geoffrey giggled as his boy toy's hand slid into his lap under the table.

"I don't know. It just bothers me." I shrugged. It was the truth, after all, though I knew I should have a better answer. "It's unnatural, and now they are fucking *everywhere*. I wouldn't complain if they went back to whatever shadows they came out of."

Tony smiled. His eyes glazed over. I didn't know if it was from some illicit substance in his blood or the way the girls were simultaneously sucking on his ears. "So long as none of them bite your neck, what do you care?" Liza moved to his neck. "Unless you ask, of course."

I rolled my eyes. "You guys are ridiculous." My patience broke. I pushed away from the table and went to the bar to escape.

Ordering a whiskey sour, I hunched my shoulders to shield myself against the rest of the bar. Why did I even stay? But where the hell else would I go? I had chained myself to this continuous replay of events, unable to tear myself from it out of...what? Fear of change? Lack of desire to adapt? I guess the boring feeling at the bar was less so than the one at my apartment.

"You look like a man who wants to buy a girl a drink."

It took me a couple of moments to realize that the husky voice was speaking to me, and I turned to see a woman sitting on the stool to my right, watching me with patient intent. In fact, I still might not have believed she was talking to me if not for the perfectly manicured hand she laid on my arm. It sent a ripple through my spine, and for a speechless moment, I just stared.

She was, in poor excuse for description, gorgeous. Every feature was exquisitely formed with black hair falling in glossy waves over her shoulders, dark eyes bearing a minimum of make-up, and very red lips that took my brain to all kinds of places it shouldn't have been going while looking at a stranger.

After that moment, though, I realized that she wasn't entirely a stranger. This was the woman watching me the night before, embedding herself in my thoughts. That bolted through the haze the previous night remained shrouded in.

She must have read my expression and liked the story it told, because those perfect lips curved in a seductive smile. She leaned toward me, and my eyes fell down the neckline of her shirt. I couldn't help myself. It was biological programming. "Cat got your tongue?"

I swallowed hard. My mouth had gone very dry. "I figured I'd better just stare for a while longer," I managed to say without stammering or gasping for air like a man just escaping strangulation. "You're a helluva sight to see."

"Aren't you a charmer?" She seemed pleased and straightened back up. "Do you remember me?"

"You'd be a damn shame to forget."

She smiled again. I felt like I was regaining my equilibrium, if slowly. It helped that my drink arrived and I drained half of it in one swallow. It dimmed the buzzing in my head and the way my eyes blurred when I looked at her, like they were melting.

"I wanted to talk to you last night, but you seemed pretty... involved with the people you were with," she continued. Every word slid from her lips, perfectly enunciated. "But you don't really look like you belong here."

Now her words snapped my attention away from her mouth, surprised by what she said. "What do you mean?"

She rolled her shoulders in a fluid movement, an elegant shrug with the deeply tanned skin of her shoulders bare but for a pair of thin straps. "If you pay close enough attention, you can just tell these things."

I tried to figure out her game by eyeing more than her cleavage, but nothing came to mind and I kept getting distracted by the little things, like her lips and her skin and her shoulders and her eyes. "It's what I have." I knew that sounded defensive, but it was also the only answer I had. She spoke words to match what I felt. I just never realized it was so obvious. "I guess you were paying pretty close attention."

"I was." She didn't say anything else about it and let that just hang in the air between us for a few moments. "I know a place more…suited to conversation. Free of mindless droning and monotony. Want to go for a ride?"

Several parts of my brain screamed that I really shouldn't go anywhere with her, but louder parts screamed that this was just what I was looking for: something new.

I finished my drink and tossed some money on the bar. "Yeah. Yeah, I do."

Chapter Three

I had no idea what I was doing when I followed her out of the bar. I felt the way the stares of my friends burned into my back, but I ignored them. Who cared what they thought anyway? The glinting eyes alone were enough to keep me entirely wrapped up in the woman leading me. She was just under a foot shorter than I was, but we both knew who had all the power.

As we left the artificial darkness and heart-regulating bass beat behind for the warm streets, I stuffed my hands in my pockets and looked at her. "So, do you have a name to go along with all that sex appeal?"

"Cielle," she replied, lips curving around the word as she smiled and didn't even bother looking in my direction, yet I couldn't escape the feeling of her focus being wrapped sinuously around me. I followed like a dog on a leash, though one who noticed the way her shoulder blades and spine shifted. Her shirt had no back to speak of, so why not enjoy the view?

"Amazing name." It took effort, but I managed to put my attention back on the sidewalk.

She finally tossed a look over her shoulder. "What's yours?"

My mouth was dry, but I could still speak. "D."

Her brows rose as she turned forward again. "I like a man with a little mystery to him."

I would be the last person to tell her that was the only mystery about me. If she thought I was mysterious and intriguing, I was going to ride that train as far as it would take me. As soon as she realized I was boring, this odyssey would end, and I wasn't ready for that to happen yet.

Her hips swung around the corner into a darker part of the street, and I experienced my first real moment of hesitation. She couldn't have weighed more than a hundred pounds soaking wet. If she tried anything short of a gun, I'm sure that I could take her, but still... There was that gut-level, evolutionary response.

It didn't take long for me to get over it. Balls over brains, as usually happens with men. She was too hot not to follow. And then when I came around the corner and saw the car she was leaning against, the last neurons in my brain hanging onto modern sensibilities vanished beneath the weight of caveman instincts.

My first car had been a heap. It had an engine that could have run the Daytona 500, but the rest of it was held together with hope and prayers. I had scraped and saved my money from my first job to get it, paying for it all my own. No matter what anyone told me, it had been a golden dream, and it had been solely mine. Now I would never claim to be a gearhead—my talents lie in other areas—but in the months leading up to my intimate purchase, I had read everything I could about that car and its predecessors. What I saw before me reignited that teenage fire and dumped jet fuel on it.

If I thought I had been wrapped around her finger before, I was now slave to this masterwork of woman and machine standing side by side.

She was temptation itself, bending over to reach into the open driver's side window. The ground-shaking hunger I could feel building within me was given a voice as the keys were in the ignition, powering up the monster of an engine. The headlights came on, blinding me in awe. What stood before me was a 1969 Chevrolet Camaro, as black as the night around us, beckoning almost as much as the femme fatale who showed it to me.

My swarthy seductress leaned back against the driver's side door, waiting with the absolute patience of one who knew what was coming next. Despite the hesitation, she knew I would follow her. She'd never had any doubt. Her arrogance had been justified, because there I was, just seconds away from drool running down my chin as my eyes desperately tried to look at the car and at her at the same time.

"Are you coming?" Her dark eyes flashed in the dim light. It was a loaded question.

"Where are we going?" I asked, even though we both knew I was getting in that car. Of course she knew; my feet betrayed me and had started me in the direction of the passenger's side door without a second thought.

"To somewhere we can talk," she replied without telling me anything and then tilted her head. "You aren't *scared*, are you?"

I was, a little, but I certainly wasn't going to *admit* it. "Of course not. You aren't anything to be scared of, right?" I flashed my most shit-eating grin, even though I wasn't so sure of the possibility of handling myself against her. This woman had power, and I'm not talking about the 8-cylinder beast thrumming between us.

Cielle laughed softly, the sound falling somewhere between a seductive chuckle and a heated purr. Any remaining surviving brain cells fried. "I suppose it's a matter of perspective, but *I* don't think I'm that frightening."

There were no more words. The temptation to ask her if I could drive swelled and deflated in an instant. This was more than a car, it was a possession, which I could tell by the care with which she opened the door and slid her electrifying legs inside. This beast had more fondness from her than I had felt for any woman, and probably ever would. It fit her like a glove.

After watching her, I felt medieval as I fumbled my way into the passenger seat. As if taunting me, she revved the engine a few times, and the whole car shimmied with the barely constrained power. She slipped it into drive in a way a part of me hoped I would find out firsthand how it felt—firm and confident. We pulled out of the alleyway and onto the modestly busy street, no sound between us but the purr of the engine and her throaty laugh of pleasure.

Streetlights and business front neon signs passed, shining an alternating rainbow spectrum on her face. I tried to hotwire my thoughts, but I couldn't seem to get past the pronounced curve of her cheekbones or the way her lips were locked in a feline smile. Every time I tried to push past it, I stalled. I could tell she knew what was going through my mind as surely as if she were feeling it herself, and it amused her to no end.

Occasionally, I managed to tear myself away long enough to glance out the window. We left the heart of the city, driving toward the outskirts. Nowhere in Adelheid actually slept at night, but it was quieter and darker out this way. Right at that moment, I didn't know if that was comforting or not, though the baser part of my consciousness felt quite at home with the idea.

She pulled into the parking lot of a bar I'd never been to and had never even heard of. Sticking the Camaro in park, she unbuckled her seatbelt and twisted slightly to face me. Being caught in that gaze was like the canary facing the cat, but I kept my brave face on. "I would have expected you to be full of questions."

I was, but her heady presence and the rarity of my misadventures thus far had kept me quiet. My sense of social self-preservation was, fortunately, well detached from the libido-driven antics thus far. "I figure it will all play out in time. Why not enjoy things as they are? I can be patient."

"That's a good trait in a man." Her smile deepened, and she climbed out of the car.

Without hesitation, I followed. Momma always said I tended to run headlong into things.

As I walked alongside her down the dirt parking lot up to a two-story Victorian with all the windows dark, I tried to figure out the place's clientele from the cars I passed but came up dry. I saw muscle cars like the one Cielle drove. I saw trucks with over-sized tires, compacts, hybrids, sedans. There was no discernable pattern, so I moved on to studying the building. The observant cynic within bailed me out of looking completely like the lapdog following its master around and let me regain my focus on what I was getting into. Keeping my eyes unglued from her wasn't a bad thing at the moment either.

The building itself looked like it had once been a house. It was well-maintained, but nothing made it stand out. The sign was wooden, hung from an old-fashioned wrought iron frame, painted white with a simple *5* in red.

"The name of the place is Five?" I couldn't keep the dubious tone from my voice.

"It is," she agreed. "It has special meaning to the owner." I waited for more, but none was forthcoming. I considered prying but realized it didn't really matter that much and I might be bound to learn why anyway.

There was no bouncer at the door or corded-off waiting line with a string of people waiting to get in. In we walked, down a short dark corridor into a dark room. It was far darker than I was used to, but I could just make out shapes of people. No music and no dancing. Everyone just sat around. A faint metallic tang hung in the air as she led me to the bar.

Behind it stood a mountain, or maybe it was a man. It moved. It turned out to be a man after all. He had to be 6'6" or maybe more, practically as broad through the shoulders and chest as he was tall. His skin was so dark he blended into the background, except when he moved his eyes or flashed a smile, which he did when Cielle leaned over the polished wood toward him.

"It's always good to see you." It wasn't a voice so much as a rumble, like a volcano contemplating eruption. He leaned forward, and they kissed cheeks. My eyes slowly adjusted, and he swung his bald head in my direction. "Who's your friend?"

"This is D." She turned toward me and waved me forward. I obeyed. "D, this is Quintus."

Quintus, 5, it made sense now. "Hey," I greeted with a nod, feeling singularly eloquent in that moment, but I didn't want to let either of them see how uneasy this place made me. My general sense that I could handle myself was shaky at best. There was something in the air that made me feel like eyes were on me, though when I glanced around, I could just about tell that no one had any interest in myself or Cielle.

"Well said." I saw by a flash of his eyes that he turned back to her. "Let me guess—backroom? Less likely to be interrupted."

"Please," she said.

"It's all yours."

I kept away from the scant few occupied tables as I trailed her down a short hallway beneath a staircase. The well-dressed door at the end was opened and revealed a room decked in opulence and old-world treasures. The opulence was not hideous or gaudy but lent an age to the house that spoke of a deep-seated history.

Cielle crossed the room ahead of me and stood before a mahogany chaise, watching as I stood just inside the doorway, looking around for a moment before turning to her.

"Why did you bring me here?" I finally had to ask a question. I had done well to avoid it for this long, but now the time had come to be an ass. "I mean, if you're after me for a good time, this hardly looks like the room for it. A cheap motel would be fine, or even a remote back road if you're okay with getting the back seats a little wet."

She chuckled, poised watchfully like a sultry sentry. "And if I wanted more than flash-in-the-pan romance?"

"Then there's coffee and old books, or my place and a threat to behave. The way you walk and the way you talk, I'd be on my best damned behavior." Mostly. "So I ask again: why here? With the dim lights and the old friend tending bar, why a backroom that looks like if I break something in a fit of passion, I'm going to be in debt until I die?"

She shrugged slightly, stepping toward me with the click of her heels on the hardwood floors. "Because it's a comfortable place, for people like me," she explained. Those clicks suddenly seemed louder.

The phrase 'people like me' gave me a chill. "People like you?"

She smiled, flashing a pair of neatly pointed fangs, and I figured it out. The sexy airs, the well-kept car, the old-word style that was out of place in this day and age.

Hell, the interest in me from the get-go was enough.

I should've seen that one coming.

Chapter Four

They say that hindsight is always 20/20, and that was most assuredly true for me at that moment, because the clues had been there: her otherworldly beauty and unnatural heights of sex appeal. I hadn't asked any questions, because I hadn't wanted the answer. And now that I had the answer, I didn't like it. I wanted to bolt, but I doubted I'd make it far. Well, bitch would at least get a fight out of her meal.

"Maybe I'll skip that second drink, after all," I said quietly, moving toward the door. First try was diplomatic enough, would at least give me a fighting chance and some momentum if she got nasty. Yet even as I did, I moved slowly, like I was waiting for her to stop me.

I was tangled in a paradox. I didn't want to be in a room alone with a vampire, but I wanted to be in that room with *her*. And it wasn't my crotch sounding off for me. She genuinely intrigued me. Even more so now. Why would a fang lure me out of a packed throb-house in front of witnesses just to feed? Why would she stalk me for two nights unless she honestly had an interest in me? Why did the idea of not knowing her bother me more than what she was?

Predictably, she stopped me. Predictably, I let her.

"You don't really want to leave, do you?" She didn't have to move, or grab my arm, or jump in front of me. The sultry tone of her voice was all the force she needed, and I was stuck in place with my hand on the doorknob, left unturned. "You know and I know that you would much rather be here with me."

"I'm not exactly a fan of fangs." My voice hardened, and my focus shifted from the battle in my head to the temptation standing behind me. I stayed facing the door, feeling that my long-stated opinions needed some token resistance or I was just a big damned hypocrite. Deep down, I knew it was more the latter than the former. What did I have to lose, really? A job I hated and an end to the monotony that happened night after night?

"You're better off going out the window than the door, then." Her tone was casual, but I had already figured out I was going to look like a walking, talking aperitif if I went out there without her protection and didn't move quickly. Still, her words were a reminder of that and I was seriously thinking about the window. Then again, where the hell would I go? Walking or running would just make me more sport and dead tired—literally.

I let the knob go and turned around but didn't move closer to her. I folded my arms across my chest and tried not to be distracted by the cut of her shirt and the look in her eyes. "Then we go back to square one. What do you want with me? If it's a meal, then let's get the fight over with. If it's something else, then you must be crazy. I'm not worth the trouble."

She smiled again but spared me the show of teeth this time. "Let's just say that I sensed a kindred spirit and felt compelled to rescue you."

"Rescue me?" That was hardly the answer I was looking for. Though honestly, I didn't have a damned clue what kind of answer I expected. Maybe more taunting and threatening, like a villainess vampire should do.

"Oh, please, you are not so naive that you believe you really belong with those people?" Somehow, she managed to be insulting and complimentary at the same time, and I found that impressive. What was more impressive was how she seemed to think of me as different from the crew I had left behind at Phoenix, after having only watched me from afar. "They're living in a murky bog of banality, where the only excitement is when they trip and try not to drown. You're better than they are."

Shreds of modesty urged me to deny it, but in that moment, she tore away a cover from thoughts I'd been having just an hour before. There was something about being laid bare in just a few words that can set the world on its ear. I stared at her, not in the lust and hunger I had been feeling most of this insofar bizarre night, but with the subtle weighing and considering that she might be telling me the plain and simple truth. I didn't know what to say, mostly because I didn't want to believe her but didn't want to sound childish and too modest. I *wanted* her to be right, that I *was* a different element from those that had mired me in their 'bog of banality.'

"So let's say you're right, that I am a different shade than those grayed-out jokes." My own venom in their description shocked a part of me, but my mouth worked without guidance. "What makes it a problem for you to fix?"

She took another step toward me. The word *stalking* bounced around in my head. I just watched her.

"You know it's true. I saw it in your eyes last night and again tonight. You looked like a man in a cage, quietly tolerating your prison but still wishing to escape and find that something more that's on the other side."

She wasn't wrong. I had never heard that fangs could read people's minds, so I must have been a walking infomercial for my dissatisfaction with the world around me. I wasn't sure if that was comforting or not, but then again, I didn't care. I hadn't cared for a long time. My heart raced and my breathing grew shallow. With each step closer she took, I felt a little more adrenaline surge with that instinctive fight-or-flight response. I *wanted* her to come at me. I wanted that fight to feel alive for once, even if it was for a brief flash before she tore my neck apart.

She took my silence as agreement. "That's why you came with me tonight," she went on. She was close enough to touch me, tantalizingly close, though she didn't need to touch me to make me feel electric. "I *saw* you. I'm the first person who has in a long time, and you knew it. You wanted to find out more. You wanted to know me more. You want to know more about what I saw."

"You seem to think an awful lot of yourself," I finally managed to say, my voice hoarse, but with half a trademark grin on my lips.

"I generally have sound reason to." She smiled. "Have I said anything so far that is untrue?"

I had to give her that one. "No." I didn't like how hungry that sounded. It tipped my hand.

Her small fingers finally rose and rested on my chest. That electric feeling cascaded like lightning over my skin. "I can show you a whole new world."

That caught me off guard, and I laughed. I kind of felt bad for doing it, especially when a startled, almost hurt, look flashed through her eyes. I still couldn't help it. "You aren't about to start singing a Disney song, right?"

Cielle frowned. Apparently, she'd been fanged before the nineties and missed out on that one. Before she could say anything, I shook my head and waved the joke away like a stale breath. "Nothing, forget it." Still frowning, it looked like I'd broken her flow. She'd had this whole line going on, and I'd just trampled all over it.

I couldn't say I felt bad. It made me feel like I was on more solid ground again, and I needed that.

She didn't take too long to recover and managed to pull a faint smile out of it. It felt more real than the sultry airs she had lured me here with, and something about that made me feel even more solid in my line of thinking. "You're a rather strange man, D, but I like you anyways."

"Why?" I pressed, because now seemed like the time to start taking back ground in this pitched conversational battle. "I get what you said before, but that still doesn't answer the question. Why do you care? Is this some kind of fang altruism? Find a human who is bored with his life and rescue him, until *you* get bored with *him*? I've read the books."

"I can see in you that you're smart enough to not believe fiction for truth, so if you're trying to get me mad, it won't work." She smiled wryly. "Although seeing you engaged in any feeling is better than how you looked at that club."

I managed to stop a knee-jerk reply and think about her words. Upon reflection, I couldn't deny that I *felt* more in that moment than I had in a long time. Here I was, lured (albeit willingly) by a fang to a secluded fang club for what I thought was going to be my last conversation on earth. I should have been scared out of my mind, or kicking and screaming, but instead I was...eager. Enthralled at the chance of testing myself against something, anything. My annoyance with the commonality of my life never really seemed to count as a worthy feeling to me. Still, my mind was mixed up. There was suspicion, uncertainty, intrigue, lust. It was a heady mix. I wasn't high, but the feelings almost made me feel like I was.

Grasping for ground again, I asked another question. "What do you want with me?"

Cielle smiled slowly. It was that expression that wrapped around me the tightest, holding me as surely as a set of iron shackles bolted to the floor. "I want you. I want to get to know you and see just what kind of man comes out of that opened cage."

"You sure that's what you want? I may not be a fang, but I'm certainly not keen on being handled." My defiant smirk returned, because it felt like good armor against the way she made my head swim and my senses submerge. "I may not be worth the trouble."

"I think there's a great deal more to know and to learn," she replied so effortlessly I almost believed it myself, though I'd argue the point out of sheer pigheaded stubbornness. "Come on, why don't you just give me the benefit of the doubt? I could get you that drink." She was persistent, I'd give her that. "Something more palatable than blood, I assure you."

The world 'blood' snapped the détente we had been negotiating through our subtle maneuvers of conversation—mine as subtle as a bull in a china shop. The word reminded me of where I was and who I was with, forcing the threads of uncertainty into threads of fear. I was surrounded by fangs, but I felt relatively confident I could make an escape if I moved fast enough. I hoped that no one would jump me since they were all too scared of something fucking up Cameron's Law.

"That's it. I'm gone," I said, stepping away from her. My back bumped the door. "My game's not with your crowd, even if it is 'stepping back in a cage'." I grabbed the door handle and fumbled it open, attempting my escape. I heard her call after me, but I kept walking until I was outside again in the fresh air, leaving the metallic scent behind me.

I knew what it was now. It was the scent of blood.

Chapter Five

It wasn't until I was in the parking lot that I remembered Cielle had driven. Since I couldn't go back in there, for many reasons, I started walking. Fortunately, I hit the main road soon and was able to grab a taxi back to Phoenix, where I picked up my own clunker and went home.

Once there, I couldn't sit still. I sat at the computer, checked my email, kept getting up to get things and then forget what I was looking for. I sat back down and tried to submerge myself in a few games, but I couldn't focus. I tried the television. I even tried to read a book, but I couldn't keep myself in one place. Ants had crawled under my skin, and I kept shifting, fidgeting and needing to move.

I kept thinking about Cielle and then told myself not to think about her, which ended about the way you'd expect. Like the little kid who gets told not to do something, it just made me want to do it more. Since the only person guiding me was me, it made it even harder.

The woman was a fang, and I didn't need to get mixed up with fangs. I told myself, more than once, that fangs were sneaky and creepy. They were dead, for heaven's sake. It was unnatural. They had all kinds of freaky abilities and liked to keep secrets. A fang could break me in half without blinking. There was no reason for me to be around them unless I wanted to be drained and buried.

Yeah, this was really helping me to calm the fuck down.

None of it worked. All I could do was mentally pour

over how beautiful and sexy and alluring she was. She was a deadly animal, but I was drawn to the exotic implications of...her. Her words bounced against the inside of my skull until my head wanted to shatter to pieces. I finally dragged myself to bed long after midnight, exhausting myself with my inner turmoil.

Even in my dreams, I couldn't escape her. Her eyes and lips and body followed me there, saying the same things over again, and each word dug deeper than it had the first time. She only grew more desirable and now unattainable, so by the time I woke up, I felt like I hadn't slept at all.

I got through work that day much like a zombie, minus the desire to eat other people's brains. Granted, it was a near thing a couple of times, but mostly because of the repetitive ignorance and incompetence of others than by some stricken sense of undeath.

By evening, I was determined to live as normally as possible and push the night before as far out of my head as I could. It frequently seemed impossible, but I was determined. Fuck this, I was determined to out-stubborn anything that bothered me this fucking much. I resisted the very thought of her every time she came into my mind.

After work, I dragged my worn ass home. I spent some time as a drone to my game of choice, ate dinner, showered, dressed, and went to Phoenix well after dark. It's what I usually did, after all, and I was focused on my life proceeding exactly as it had before. I didn't think about Cielle's words and instead wanted my normalcy. I had chosen this and so this was what I was going to do.

I found Tony and one of his girls at the usual table, along with Geoffrey and some new guy. I didn't see Raven anywhere, so I sat down and we all exchanged the usual round of "hey" that served as a greeting.

"Who'd you leave with last night?" Maria asked, her head leaning on Tony's shoulder while he stared off at the gyrating dance floor.

"Just some girl," I replied as casually as I could, shrugging. I didn't really want to talk about it.

That answer seemed to satisfy her and she went back to saying things only Tony could hear. Geoffrey didn't seem to care one way or the other, too engrossed in his evening's conquest. I considered going to the bar for a drink or tripping a passing waitress, but instead I stared at the four of them. Was it always like this? We didn't, any of us, *talk*. Words were occasionally spoken, but we just wrapped ourselves in whatever malignant substance helped drown out the monotony and allowed our minds to hallucinate the night away, making it feel okay to be this...inactive. Before that night, it had been Raven I sunk my attention into, and she certainly qualified as malignant.

Somewhere in my head, a buzzing started. I listened to the grating music shaking the soles of my feet against the floor and the strange mumbled words of the people I sat with and the people around me. It started annoying me, in the deep-down, nails-on-chalkboard kind of way. It was like for the first time I realized how miserable this all really was.

Just twenty minutes ago, I'd been convincing myself I wanted this because I had chosen it. Now, I couldn't for the life of me resign myself to this shadow of a life.

I couldn't look at them anymore and turned away, sending my eyes out around the club and over the dance floor. My eyes fell on Raven, plastered against the same goofy-looking bastard, swaying in time to the music. I guess you really couldn't call it music, but it was the closest thing they had here. Between the music, the dancing, and the douche she was with, I had to imagine she was high on something. She didn't look drunk. I watched for a while, but she never noticed. I guess it wasn't all that different from when we were...whatever we were.

Finally turning away, I realized the air started closing

in. I had never been claustrophobic, but this had to be what it felt like. Everything began to feel too tight, like the room was steadily getting smaller, or maybe the world was. My breathing got shallow, and I began to feel a very strong need to do something. Whether it was flip over a table or run screaming into the night, I didn't know, but it had to happen and it had to happen *soon*, or I was going to explode.

"D, man, are you okay?" I was surprised that Geoffrey managed to tear himself away long enough to notice. Then I wondered just how I looked from the outside that made him worry.

"Yeah, I'm fine." Even to my own ears, my voice sounded hoarse. "I just need some air." My body had tensed so much with the desperate need to escape that my muscles felt rigid when I tried to move them, pushing up from the table and walking out without saying anything more to anyone.

It got a little better once I was outside, but the open air didn't help nearly as much as I wanted it to. I don't know what I hoped would happen, but it wasn't happening, and it almost made the anxiety worse.

Standing on the sidewalk, I looked at the people walking by. Half of them didn't look back and the other half looked at me like I might be crazy. Maybe they were right, because I certainly *felt* crazy.

The buzzing had receded into my old friend the hunger, that driving need I didn't know how to fill. It had gotten tangled up with whatever I had been feeling inside the club and now the two held onto each other inside my head, pushing me to something, but I still didn't know what. It was maddening, and I didn't know how to stop it. I could only feel it.

I started walking, because I had to *do* something. Without any direction in mind, my feet chose for me and brought me to my car. I got in and turned over the engine. My music player started with a song from the nineties that it hadn't played in a while. The music began to force my swirling thoughts to slowly coalesce into something resembling coherence, although I ignored whatever that final product was. My breathing was hard and I tried to regulate it, force it, control it. It helped me focus, and the music soothed the savagery that was on a rampage inside.

Pulling out onto the road, I just started driving. I listened to the music and drove on some back-of-my-mind autopilot.

It wasn't until I put the car in park that I realized where that autopilot had taken me. When the thought dawned on me, I just sat there, staring in a mild disbelief. My thumbs drummed on the steering wheel as I turned it over in my mind, trying to see if this was some sort of strange game or if this really was my subconscious's guidance. The idea of external influence occurred to me, though if external influence *had* been working on me, you'd think it would have worked long before now with more drastic results. No, this was classic subconscious, to be sure.

It didn't matter if I kept my headlights on or not, so I turned them off. Outside, the white sign with the red number *5* swayed in the wind.

Chapter Six

I didn't bother to consider turning back. I had already gotten myself out of here once with my skin intact, so odds were I could do it a second time. Then again, odds said I wouldn't be struck by lightning.

A sprinkling of raindrops spattered the windshield. Well, shit.

Honestly, I didn't consider turning back because the hunger quieted when I thought of Cielle. Her words haunted me, no matter how stubbornly I tried to snuff them out. I gave in. When I did, the hunger began to sate itself with feeding off the knowledge of where I was going.

I had parked in the back and got out, starting the walk up to the entryway like a doomed man hitting the whorehouse. The cynic in me said that my odds were good I'd be food soon anyway, so why not walk into it with my head up and my balls made of steel? That did nothing to calm the nervous crawl of my skin or the sour pit in my stomach, but I'd long ago figured out a way to pass myself off as completely in control when I was in over my head. Part of my knack for observing folks and emulating them when I didn't feel it, I guess.

I walked in and didn't have a pack of fangs lunging for my jugular. Score one for my side. I realized once the dark recesses of the club engulfed me that I really had no basis for presuming Cielle was here. I guess I just had a feeling or figured maybe the bartender would know where I could find her. They seemed to be friendly. Now that I had it in mind to find her, I'd do whatever I needed to.

Fate or luck or some twisted mind control was in my favor; I found Cielle sitting at the bar with a glass in her hands. I didn't have to get too close to know what it was, and that was enough to twist my stomach further, but I pushed past it. I thumped down on a barstool beside her without preamble, not even looking, and met Quintus's look with a sure one of my own. "Whiskey sour and make it strong." Beside me, her lips curved in that slow smile.

"I didn't think I'd see *you* again," she said, her voice a purr. It was quiet in this bar, so she didn't have to shout to be heard. That was nice.

"I didn't think you'd see me again either," I replied, taking up the tumbler Quintus put in front of me and gulping down half of it. I didn't have a plan, but fuck plans. This whole bizarre week hadn't been planned, so why mess with it? Folding my arms on the bar, I inhaled slowly. "Maybe I had a change of heart. Or maybe I liked seeing you in a skirt. Maybe I just wanted to see that car of yours." Part of me wanted to get ultra-nervous about which fangs were looking at me like their next *grande* happy meal. The other part of me was too arrogant to care. The whiskey sour hit my empty stomach quick and helped out the arrogant side.

Cielle rested her hand on my arm. My skin lit up with goosebumps, and it felt...good. Despite what I knew she was, I was still enticed by her. She was attractive to me, and she was interested in me. No man can really resist that, no matter if she sprouts bat wings and stalks the night. She leaned toward me. Tonight, she wasn't slicked out in slutty clubbing attire, but instead in a more refined and elegant long skirt and shirt. It made her even more attractive. "You don't look very comfortable. Would privacy help?"

I wanted to say yes so I could get rid of the wariness. I wanted to say no because I wasn't completely convinced I could trust myself alone with this woman. Ultimately, I decided one fang was better than a room full of them. "Yeah. Less eyes on me would be good." I pounded back the rest of my drink and slid off the barstool at the same time she did. I let her lead, though I didn't linger behind as we strode back to the room I had eagerly fled the night before.

The door clicked shut behind me, and I focused less on the old-world accoutrements and more on the woman that had drawn me here. "What changed your mind?" she asked as she moved past me to the couch, letting her fingertips trail over my upper arm as she did so. She arranged her skirt just-so as she sat, awaiting my reply as impassively as my high school literature teacher.

I stood there, thinking it over. I could admit my subconscious had drawn me here, which might tip my hand early and let her know she had more power over me than I wanted. I could confess to the blatant displeasure I had with my life now that she had calmly and cleanly pointed out all the flaws in it I had tried to ignore. I could have come up with some excuse about forgetting my wallet or phone or God knew what else, but that would just be utterly lame.

So, I went with the classic male response. And what followed was a complete fuckup of my entire plan. Well, like I said, fuck plans.

"I don't know." I stuffed my hands in my pockets to keep from waving them around. "Maybe I couldn't stop thinking about what you said last night. I tried to get through my usual day and went back to the club. It all felt so...miserable and boring. I was there all of five fucking minutes before I wanted to tear my hair out. I left and just started driving. I ended up here."

"I guess we'll take that as a sign, then." She managed to say it without sounding like the world's greatest egotist, and I had to give her credit for that.

"Yeah. But a sign to what?" My feet had led me this far, but now they abandoned me. I was glued in place, unwilling to move forward but unwilling to leave. "You got a sign to tell me what the fuck it is I'm looking for?"

She picked up on the feet-nailed-to-the-floor routine, getting back up off the couch and moving toward me. She took it slow, like someone sneaking up on an animal they didn't want to get away. She held out her hand, palm toward me, and waited. A chill went through my body, part exhilaration at not knowing what was coming next and part pure fear this was some sort of invitation straight to hell. I couldn't just let her stand there with her hand out, not when I had come this far on my own and placed myself squarely in this new experience.

I reached up and pressed my hand to hers, and our fingers interlocked. It was so simple a gesture, not revealing intimacy or anything other than the smallest effort of trust, but warmth suffused my body from my fingertips outward, just from holding her hand. She gestured to the couch with the slightest tilt of her head, and I only nodded, unable to say a word, thanks to my quickened pulse and labored breath. I tried very hard to hide the latter by forcing myself to breathe in and out through my nose. Our hands untwined, and I sat with her beside me, her arm resting across the back of the seat, lightly against my shoulders.

Cielle smiled again. "Tonight, I think you came looking for me." It didn't take a genius to figure that one out. "I can offer you something those others can't. I'm not like anyone else you know."

Part of my natural inclination was to argue her down from her opinion of herself, but I couldn't without making myself a liar. Besides, she was intoxicating when she sat that close and leaned toward me that way. "No, you're not." I couldn't help but concede her point. "Although when I spent all that time wishing for something interesting to happen, spending time around fangs was nowhere on my list."

"I suppose you just haven't known enough *vampires*,"

she said with clear emphasis. Her voice lowered to a husky, breathless tone as she leaned closer, until her lips pressed against mine. It was faint, skin brushing skin, but lights exploded behind my eyelids, and I felt lightheaded. I half-leaned forward, wanting more, but she pulled back, not going far but remaining enough out of reach to make the hunger in me stir again. "I can give you what you've been looking for," she whispered hotly against my face.

The black hole of my hunger began a deep roar from within, and I swear to God, time slowed as she moved toward my neck. It was hot, for a moment, but when my mind caught up and remembered what she was, I tensed and jerked away. She caught my gaze sidelong and smiled with mild admonishment. "Relax," she purred. She didn't say anything that would convince me to do that, but I did it anyways. The fear and adrenaline of what she was, mixed with my desire and eagerness to keep her touching me, produced a sweet cocktail unlike anything I had before experienced. Something about her voice just grabbed me by the soul and shook me hard. Trust. If she had wanted to feed on me, she could have done it already.

I was beginning to *trust* a fang.

When she kissed my neck and I felt no trace of teeth, I relaxed and let her wash me under with everything that was *her*.

If you're reading this and thinking I was a total sucker, then you would be thinking correctly. She was gorgeous and all over me. I couldn't help myself, because aside from that inherent fang issue, there was nothing else stopping me. Compared to her, I had only known bare imitations of desire and passion, frail mockeries that had lain in the way until both were spent. This was intensity and wanting, something I had never felt directed at me before.

As I pulled her closer, the restlessness in my mind eased. The depths of my personal hunger were muted with a new voracity that was entirely for Cielle. Higher brain function was now for the weak. Everything dissolved into need, hands that could not hold on tight enough, bodies that could not be close enough. To hell with the reality lying in wait on the other side of the door. All that mattered was her and I, feeding and tightening that connection between us.

The world dissolved into her for an eternity.

Afterward, sweat clung to my back and cooled quickly, but that really didn't matter in the shade of sated lust. Leaning my head down next to hers, I inhaled her exotic scent and let myself remain lost for a while. All other feelings stopped while I was with her. She was kissing my shoulder and neck. Overwhelmed in sensation, I didn't even notice the faint prick against my skin.

Her fingers tangled in my hair and drew my head up. Her bottom lip was sunk under her teeth as she leaned up and kissed me again. I thought, briefly, that I tasted something metallic. Damned if it mattered, as again I got lost too quickly in the passionate way she kissed me.

Nothing seemed to matter in those moments. I can't even accurately describe just how total my immersion in this woman was and the things I missed because of it. All that mattered was her and the way she pulled back and looked at me, the way she had both hands in my hair. I noticed, briefly, a faint trickle of blood on her lip, but it didn't process.

I can still remember the look of absolute pleasure on her face, and I knew it was because of me.

Then the bitch snapped my fucking neck.

Chapter Seven

I woke up.

That night, that simple statement had a great deal more meaning than it did any other night of my life. It happened slowly, like I was a wall being built brick by brick, as I dragged myself into the conscious world. Something was different, but my primitive monkey brain had yet to figure out exactly what that was. For a brief moment, I thought perhaps I'd had a bizarre dream and it was a night like any other.

I inhaled deeply, and it felt different. Looking down, I saw I didn't have any clothes on, but I wasn't cold. But it was summer. I tried to remember what I did last night, and it came back to me in bits and pieces. I remembered that gnawing feeling in my mind that drove me out of Phoenix and brought me to 5. I remember talking to Cielle and feeling the heat, feeling her.

She kissed my neck. She kissed my mouth. It tasted strange. Putting her hands on my head, she twisted…

She broke my fucking neck.

Everything came to a screeching halt. I gingerly touched my teeth with the tip of my tongue and found two of them to be noticeably sharper than they had been the night before. My hand rose to my chest, feeling for that familiar sensation of life. Nada. Frantically, I checked both of my wrists and my neck, but to no avail.

I sat up like a shot, flicking my gaze around the room like a spotlight during a prison break. I was looking for one thing and one thing only, damn the fact it wasn't the same room I had died in. Yeah. I died.

My eyes fell on her sitting in a chair in the corner. She looked nervous. *She damn well should be nervous*, I thought.

"You. Bitch," I growled, with more venom and rage than any shouting match I had ever been in. I stared her down, and the look of fear became panic. Much of the confidence that must have taken her through the first act was now long since gone, though she wasn't quaking. "You *killed* me and made me a fucking fang. *What in the fuck did you DO!*"

Holding my temper had never been my strong suit, but it had been even worse when I was younger. Now it seemed all of that self-control had died along with my body last night. The hunger was there, clawing at my insides even harder now after being so sated last night. It howled at me, fanning the flames of my anger and keeping me from regaining any semblance of composure.

I got up and exploded, turning to fling the mattress off of the bed in a desperate attempt to vent this blinding fury. Being the newly unliving had its advantages, at least. It was a heavy mattress, but I flipped it like a trashcan lid. It crashed against the dresser on the other side of the room. Cielle jumped up but stood her ground. "D, you have to calm down—"

"Calm down? *Calm down?* What did you fucking do to me, you crazy bitch?"

"I turned you." Already she looked as though she had her regrets. "I had to do it," she breathed.

I wouldn't have heard her before, but apparently being dead gave you wonderful new insights. Hearing a murmur from across the room as I made some satisfying crashing noises was surreal.

The mirror shattered, and I stared at my distorted reflection. I can still see it. It must be a joke, I thought. It couldn't be real, could it?

I checked my pulse again, tracing my hand against the veins in my arm. As before, there was no subtle thump-thump to reassure me I was among the living. Given the commotion I was causing, my heart should have been going a mile a minute.

It crashed into the chilling comprehension that I was dead now.

It fed a storm in my mind that couldn't be subdued.

I was a fang.

I was a fucking *vampire*.

If someone had asked me what the last thing in the world I would want to happen to me would be, this would have been a close second to becoming a brain-eating zombie.

I should have seen it coming. You couldn't trust a damned fang. Why else would someone like *her* be so hard after someone like me?

Now, I was one of them, and I knew enough to know there was no going back. It was live this way or set myself on fire.

"Fucking—" I started to shout, but the heights of my anger caused a logjam of whatever epithets were going to spring forth next. I started stomping around the room, looking for my clothes. They were surprisingly hard to find, but I think it was because my vision was angrily blurry. "I can't fucking believe you did this to me. You had no goddamned right."

"D, please, listen to me." Cielle hurried over, heedless of my anger. That just pissed me off more. "I had to do it. I need your help, and you couldn't help me as a human."

"This is rich," I snapped. "You *murder* me and then are going to ask for a favor?" I laughed coarsely, struggling with my pants. "I don't fucking care why or how you did this. What the fuck am I supposed to do now? I ought to tear your fucking throat out." I gritted teeth that didn't fit together the same way anymore, turning on her in a flash and causing her to back up just out of reach. "You had no fucking right!"

"I needed you!" she shouted back defiantly. Her own fangs were long and sharp, and she stormed back into my face. "I still need you. If you would stop your fucking primordial ranting for one minute, you might let me explain why."

"I'm not listening to another Goddamned word of yours," I said, shoving my finger in her face for emphasis. "I'm getting the fuck out of here. Fuck's sake, it's not even the same night, is it? I don't fucking care. This is un-fucking-believable."

I'd always been a night owl. Now it was permanent, and I couldn't help but think it more sinister. I could never see the sun again. Not that I'd been a fan of it before, but the fact I didn't even have the option now bothered me on some deep evolutionary level.

Finding my shirt, I thrust my arms into the sleeves, grabbing up my boots from where they had been stashed under the bed.

"Please," she tried again in a pleading tone, following me over to where I sat to stuff my feet inside. She reached out to touch my arm, but I stopped and gave her a baleful glare that made her retract it. I could barely hear her over the sound of my fury. "It's a matter of life and death! Would you just stop for one fucking moment and listen to me?"

"No!" I roared, the sound and force of which brought me to my feet. She backed up again, clearly terrified. I could almost taste her fear, and something dark inside me fed on it. My rage grew, and I advanced on her. "You have given me jack shit of a reason to listen to you or to trust you for an instant." Shadows grew over my vision. "You fucking *murdered* me and turned me into something I never wanted to be!" I lunged for her, but something grabbed me with the strength of a tree.

I struggled blindly, tearing one arm out of an iron-like

grasp before it was grabbed again. The tips of my teeth tore the inside of my lower lip.

"Stop!" A mountain rumbled behind me, and somewhere in my brain, I knew it was Quintus holding me back. That didn't stop me. I was lifted off the ground and thrown toward the door. The big Black vampire inserted himself between us. "Stop," he repeated.

Old human instincts made me breathe hard as I considered trying to plow around him and get to her, but something finally turned over in my mind. Instead, I just spoke through my teeth, meeting her eyes as best I could around the blockade. "You never asked if it was something I ever might consider, never even suggested the possibility in order for us to be together." Turning, I grabbed the doorknob and tore it open, nearly off the hinges all together. "I'm fucking *done* with you."

No one tried to stop me on my way out and the better for them. I would have torn apart anyone who tried.

My only piece of good luck for the evening was that I'd driven myself the night before, so my car was still there. My keys were still in my pocket, so at least she hadn't tried to trap me.

I was a fang. A part of my brain had latched onto that and acknowledged it, and as you could imagine, that part was none too pleased. Another part of me didn't believe it and thought the lack of heartbeat and needing to breathe was just some trick of my imagination. It was surreal. Nothing looked the way it had before. Driving home was a bizarre experience where every light was too bright and every sound was too loud.

Dealing with the recurring anger and violation alongside the overwhelming heightening of my senses distracted me from something I nearly missed until I got home; it was a shrouded image in my mind of guilt. I had nothing to be guilty for and everything to be angry for, but there it sat, bugging the fuck out of my subconscious. Worst yet was the feeling that I could look over my shoulder and see the source of it, or even physically point my finger at it. Its persistence bugged the shit out of me and only kept my anger simmering.

Once I got into my apartment, I didn't know what to do with myself. It was a gnawing uncertainty and need to be moving, like a panther pacing the cage. It chewed on me and gave me the paranoid fear that now, if I stopped moving, I would stop being a fang and become fully dead. I paced every path available at hyper-speed. The slow-devouring hole in my psyche pounded and roared, banging against the bars of its cage like it never had before. And all the while, that guilt waited like a far off echo, eventually turning into…remorse?

Just to hear the satisfying crash, I threw a glass at the wall. It shattered with an impressive display of glittering shards. When I realized it didn't make me feel any better, I sunk to the floor and did nothing until dawn came and swept me under.

☾○☽

If I had thought the week I had pneumonia when I was thirteen was bad, and if I'd thought the week after my first 'true love' girlfriend broke up with me was bad, and if I'd thought the near week of constant hangovers during my first year of college was bad… I really had no idea.

My first week as a fang was worse.

I refused to leave my apartment. I didn't go into work, having just enough sense of responsibility to call and quit over the phone. After several obnoxious messages, I sent a text to all my 'friends' to tell them, in brief, that I wouldn't be seeing any of them again. None of them really understood, but how could they? None of them had the pleasant experience of being a murder victim and unwilling fang.

The only good thing was the usual hunger that plagued me was gone for that week. Unfortunately, it was replaced by another, more tenacious kind. I tried eating and drinking, but my body rejected it quickly. I became violently ill and threw it all back up. I knew what my body needed, but I didn't want it. I resisted, hard. The hunger pains were unlike anything I'd ever experienced, wracking both mind as well as body. I cannot describe them adequately. I did whatever I could to distract myself, as long as it didn't mean going outside, even at night.

I'm not sure why I couldn't bear the thought of going out into the world. It wasn't like I'd be alone, but I felt like I would be. No matter how much it hurt, or how hard the hunger drove me to go feed, I resisted. I just couldn't handle it. The very thought of going out there was, if you could believe it, more painful than the craving.

By day four, I was reduced to sucking on a cube steak two days past its use-by date. Such desperation still didn't convince me to go out. I was too ashamed. I was too frightened. Yes, I was afraid, but I didn't know what of.

☾○☽

The fifth night, I had almost given in.

The hunger was intense. I sat, staring at my apartment door from the kitchenette, debating whether or not I would kill anyone if I were to walk out that door. I had no idea what I'd do otherwise...maybe chase down a deer. Maul squirrels in the park. Each thought was sickening, but they were the only options to come to mind that weren't murder. The deep, recessed part of my fouled humanity had already begun to consider that the latter was only a problem *if I got caught.*

Yeah, no way in hell I was going out that door.

It was following that awful consideration that a knock

came. It stirred me a little from my death-stare, and it was then I noticed the buzzing that had been going on between my ears. It began to feel louder, so much so that I wondered how in the hell it hadn't driven me completely insane at that point.

The knock came again, though to be fair, it was more of a banging.

"Go away," I croaked, my voice hoarse from disuse and my condition.

Whoever was there, they didn't hear me or didn't care. The banging came again.

"Go AWAY!" I managed to shout, coming out like a deathly ill man making a last request.

"D." The voice was muffled, but I knew it all too well. It rekindled the anger I had been staving off with this nasty hunger. I pulled myself up from the cold linoleum floor and staggered toward the door.

"I said GO THE FUCK AWAY!" My voice was stronger; funny how disgusted anger could do that.

"You need me." Her response was plain, and I couldn't deny it. She had gotten me into this horrible mess, and by damn, she should be the one to get me out of it. I could... feel...her there. Guilt and anger came back at me through that door in waves. In my current state, I couldn't tell if I was imagining it or feeling it outright.

I lurched to the door, fumbled with the chain, and threw it open to let it bang off the wall.

"I don't need you." God, I was exhausted.

"You do," she said simply, and she was right. She didn't come in, instead standing her ground there in the frame. "I can help you. Please, let me help you. You look...awful."

"I'm fucking *dead*. How else am I supposed to look?" I leaned on the doorjamb, part of me wanting to cling to her like a boat in a storm. The other part wanted to find the strength to rip her apart.

She huffed an exasperated sigh. "If you won't take my help, at least let me give you a little something to say I'm sorry."

"Like what? A flea collar, because you're going to turn me into a wererat next? Or are you going to teach me how to do witchcraft and wizardry?"

She surprised me with a reflexive quickness I had not yet witnessed, her hands on my collar and jamming me back against the door. "Do you want to joke around for eternity or get a fucking grip?" There was the anger again, wide-eyed and boring into me. But something else, and damned if I could figure it out in my current state. She let go of my collar but kept her hands on my chest. "I wanted you to have something from that night, something to remind you of me." I opened my mouth for another jackass retort, but she put a finger to my lips and silenced me. "Something tangible. Something I think you honestly wanted more than me."

Peering into her eyes dubiously, it took me a minute to realize she was holding something up at eye-level. Car keys. Well, one key, really, with a simple black leather keychain attached.

"You're giving me your car to apologize?" I wasn't excited. Really, I was quite disappointed. What about a magic potion to turn me human? Seven dwarves to do my taxes and pay my bills? A fucking *car*?

She looked a little crestfallen at that. "But I thought that—"

I laughed. I honestly laughed, for the first time in a week. Hell, probably the first honest laugh in months. "God, woman, it's going to take a lot more than a car to get me to forgive you," I said ruefully.

She looked put out, but I didn't care. I stalked back into the confines of my hovel. The hunger was muted, and I could feel her eyes on my back as sure as I could feel the shirt on my shoulders.

Behind me, she sighed. "All right. All right. But I...want to make it up to you. I'll go. But please...let me help you. You may need me. But I'm going to need you more."

"Whatever. Just go."

She left.

❨O❩

Three more days, I endured like that.

Finally, I realized that unless I wanted to end it for good, I would have to do something for work or end up on the street in a really secure cardboard box. I knew fangs didn't generate body heat, but they could still freeze. It gets cold in New England. It was warm in the South, but I could never go home like this.

I'd have to go out, whether I liked it or not.

CHAPTER EIGHT

Once I got it in my head to go outside, I knew I couldn't forge my way in this new world alone. I'd need help. The only fang I knew was Cielle, but the very thought of her brought back the smoldering rage. I couldn't go see her, but the only other feasible thought left a bad taste in my mouth. I'd never liked eating crow.

I ended up on the doorstep of the Stanton Agency, because I knew the woman was known for helping people. From what I'd heard on the news, she helped both the preternatural community and the humans with preternatural issues. I now fell into that former category and had to hope. Looking and feeling like ragged hell, I figured I had enough issues to qualify.

Stumbling inside, the first sight greeting me was a surprisingly bright office and a beautiful blonde behind a desk. I guess old stereotypes in the brain made me think it would be a dark, dungeon type place with a gothic looking receptionist (like my ex) out front. I certainly hadn't expected this cheerleader type with the Midwestern features and dazzling smile turned in my direction.

"Can I help you?" she asked, pleasant and perky.

"Umm, I don't know." The words came out a little more jumbled than I would have liked. I was tired, strained, humorless. My ego was bruised beyond cleverness to make a quip or a cynical impression. I was even too tired to try hitting on her, like any newly single man in his right mind would do. Instead, I was the epitome of the disheveled and angsty loner who needed help but didn't know how to ask for it. God, I was pathetic.

Ms. Perky didn't really have a chance to respond to my dishevelment. The door behind her opened, and Stanton herself stepped out. She had her mouth open to say something to the blonde but saw me first and made her disapproval abundantly clear. "You're that jackass from the club." It wasn't a question so much as a declarative statement, and a damn accurate one. I prepared to tuck my tail between my legs and slink away.

The secretary looked up at her and then back at me. "This is *that* guy?"

"Yeah," she said, folding her arms across her chest. She started to say something more but stopped and frowned, as if picking up a bad smell. "Oh, I see."

It took me a minute to figure out what she could mean. I hadn't said a word to her yet or even explained to Blondie my plight. I knew exactly what she was, but how could she... Brows knit, I tilted my head. "You can tell?"

Stanton nodded. I realized, really for the first time, that she was actually an attractive woman. I'd call her more handsome than pretty, with a hard line to her jaw and a strong nose, but pretty blue eyes and long dark hair. "Can't be more than...what, a few days? A couple of weeks?"

"How can you tell that?"

"Give it a few years and you'll learn." She paused and looked me over from head to toe to head. "So, what can I do for you?"

My brief-lived curiosity about her fled with the return of my shame. "I don't know any fangs."

Her brows knit with a slightly sour expression for my slang. "What about the *vampire* who turned you?"

I grimaced. "I really don't want to talk to her ever again."

She frowned a little harder but didn't press. "I see." Something in her look suggested she might understand. "Madison—" She turned to the secretary. "—do I have some time here?"

"You have an appointment in thirty minutes, but you're clear until then, barring any sort of supernatural explosions which require your expertise."

Stanton grinned. "Let's see if we can avoid those."

Madison batted long, pretty lashes. "I always *try*."

Watching the two of them made me feel on the outside looking in, but it was a nice picture and almost enough to draw me out of myself. I was unused to it on a personal level, what with my sudden solitary confinement. Then again, I was really unused to it for a greater portion of my life. And it wasn't just that it was two attractive women, but the obvious shared warmth. I couldn't recall ever really having that with someone. They seemed like sisters, but they didn't look alike.

Stanton waved me to follow her into her office, shutting the door behind us as she invited me to a seat and took one behind her desk. "First things first, if you want my help, I will at least be cordial enough to stop calling you 'that jackass from the bar,' so a name would be good."

"D," I replied. A long pause stretched between us. I finally relented and gave her my full name.

"You may call me Sadie." She smiled, inclining her head. "I need to know your story. No, I don't need your autobiography. I just need to know some of the details around your turning, particularly when it was and what you've been doing since. There are no bodies to worry about, are there?"

I shook my head quickly, a bit unsettled by the thought of being under suspicion for murder when I was seeking out help on my own. "I haven't left my apartment in a week." I almost felt like a little kid talking to a grown-up. I didn't like it, but maybe it was justified. "It happened the night after that one at the club. You know, the night when I was an asshole to you for no particular reason." I had the good manners to grimace with embarrassment. "I met a girl that night. We hooked up the next night. While I was enjoying some afterglow, she bit me and then kissed me, but must have bit her lip first. Just as I realized I'd tasted blood, she broke my neck."

Sadie frowned. "Did you know she was a vampire?" I nodded. "Did you agree to be turned?" To that, I shook my head vehemently. "Well, I'm very sorry about that. It's rare these days and strictly against coven law, but not everyone obeys the rules...or ethics."

"It's not like humans are all that good at it either," I had to allow, scuffing my boot against the carpet. I had managed to push my hunger to a dull roar at the back of my mind, but it was starting to mount again. I tried to resist.

"If you want to give me her name, I can speak to Jade about it. She's the leader of the local coven and may be able to help. You could also talk to the police. You were technically murdered, but I'll warn you that since you're also walking and talking, the law is still a little murky on it."

The idea had never occurred to me, and now I was frustrated with myself for something else, but I shook my head. "I just want to put it behind me. It's done, but I'm still sort of here. I just want to move forward and not involve anyone more than I have to."

"It's your choice." I couldn't tell if she disapproved or not. She studied me and then changed the line of thought. "I don't know you, but I'm betting you normally look better than you do now. What have you been doing for the past week?"

I shrugged. "Like I said, I haven't left my apartment. I couldn't stand the idea of going out, seeing people, drinking blood...so as you can guess, I haven't eaten in a week. I doubt sucking the juice from an old steak counts for much."

"Not for much," she agreed with a sympathetic grimace. Getting to her feet, she walked to a little mini fridge in the corner. She pulled out a glass jar and unscrewed the top, handing it to me. "I don't care if you like it or not. Drink."

Although I had been sick at the thought all this time, seeing it now in front of me made my hunger break free from where I'd shoved it in my mind. The hunger moaned and growled until I couldn't hear anything else, and I reached for the glass. I lifted it to my lips, wincing like a kid about to take medicine, expecting that first taste to be revolting.

It wasn't. In fact, it was ambrosia. After the first hesitant sip, I chugged the rest of it harder than any beer I'd had in college. I might as well have had a horde of frat boys standing around me, chanting.

Embarrassed when it was done, I handed the glass back. I desperately wanted more, but she didn't look like she was going to be providing it, and I couldn't bring myself to ask. At least this took the edge off.

She set the glass away and sat back behind her desk. "Vampires can go a few days without feeding, but it should be no longer than two or three. A vampire starved of blood is not a pretty picture—no more than anyone starved—but we have a bad tendency of snapping and going into blood fevers if it goes too long."

That sounded ominous. "Blood fever?"

"Have you ever heard the term berserker?" she asked. I nodded. "Well, think of it like vampire berserkers. The brain just blows up and sees nothing but the desperate need for blood. The weakness from starvation vanishes until the need is sated. Literally, the vampire sees red."

And I felt green. It was not a pretty picture to imagine.

"You're lucky in one thing, though," she continued. "New vampires without a guiding sire often have trouble containing themselves. You must have considerable strength of will to have held on that long and then make it here to talk to me without going on a miniature rampage on the sidewalk."

"I've always been called stubborn." I smiled weakly. Before, it had been used as an insult, but now it seemed to be my salvation. She was complimenting me, and I should have been grateful, but the dull hunger—and how surreal all of this was—kept me from my unusually thankful self. Now I had to worry about a berserker rage turning me into a mass menace, and the one person who should have hated me was being incredibly nice.

It was going to be a long night.

It was going to be a long life.

Chapter Nine

I corralled my thoughts just as she smiled at me.

"In this case, it's a good thing," she said. "Hopefully, you're feeling a little better now. I wouldn't go on any blood binges, though. You can get sick from it just as a human can from over-eating or over-drinking." She paused and let that sink in. I took note. "Now, have you considered going to the Coven House? They could probably help you adjust better than I can."

The idea had never occurred to me. That was probably because I'd never heard of the Coven House until she said it, though now I realized she'd mentioned it just five minutes ago. "What's that?"

Her brows rose with surprise. "Wow, you really are a novice. Okay, well, the major powers of Adelheid have organizations. For the vampires, there is the coven. Now, Adelheid's coven doesn't require that every vampire belong to it. It is optional, but it has some benefits. It's kind of like a social club. Jade—the leader—doesn't adhere to too many of the old-world rules."

"Umm, all right." I nodded. "I'm still struggling with the idea of being around myself as a fa…as a vampire. Or being around any other vampires, really. I don't think I'm up for any vamp social clubs. Can't *you* just help me out?" I sounded pathetic and I knew it, but in for a penny, in for a pound. I had already checked any hope of masculinity at the door, so might as well be honest instead.

"I'll help you." She ran her hand through her hair, chuckling and shaking her head. "I don't know why, but I guess I'm a sucker for a hard-luck story." She rearranged some files on her desktop. "Do you have a job?"

"Not anymore. I quit in a post-murder sulk," I admitted. "It was an IT job, but I did different kinds of work while I was a teenager and in college."

She was quiet for a moment, perfectly silent and still in a way I was going to have to get used to being around. "I might have something for you."

"You don't look like you have enough equipment to need a full time IT guy troubleshooting the network or restoring the phones," I said uncertainly. I wasn't sure what else she could hire me for, and that was worrying.

Sadie smiled. "You're right, though we could use some of it on a smaller scale. No, I'm looking at six-one or six-two of broad shoulders and vampire strength. I need someone to go out with a couple of my people on jobs. They've been getting some trouble and could use a little body guarding."

"I've never done any kind of security work." She had the height and shoulders and vampire parts right, but I didn't know about the rest.

"Really, you won't need to do much. Maybe make some fang faces, scare off some kooks, or be able to dial nine-one-one on a cell phone. I just need a body to go out with some appointments and help keep an eye on things. Perhaps do some of that IT stuff around here at other times, because I suck at computers, and Madison breaks them." She paused, like she was waiting for a reply. None came, so she went on. "I'm sure I can find some other stuff for you, too. Kind of a general assistant. Won't pay a lot but could keep you supplied at the butcher's until you get the hang of the vampire thing."

I nodded, albeit uncertainly. It didn't sound that hard, and what other options did I really have? Besides, being around Sadie would help me. "Sure," I said. "What other options do I have, right?" I offered weakly, some of my humor resurfacing.

"Good." She nodded and got to her feet. "We'll go talk to Madison and get some forms filled out."

I made a note of the secretary's name, idly wondering if she ever went by Maddie.

In the front office, Madison pulled a file folder out of a desk drawer and began to give me the usual new employee forms. I had a little trouble concentrating on them and had to ask a few dumb questions, but Madison was patient with me. After all, things were moving very quickly, weren't they? Still, it would be stupid to look a gift horse in the mouth, even if the horse had long, pointy teeth.

Just as I was sitting down to start working on my tax forms, someone in an office down the hall shouted. An otherworldly roar followed. I heard a man shouting at someone to run, and some instinct drove me from my seat and down that hall, just in time to catch a man stumbling out, black smoke billowing behind him.

"Shut the door," he gasped in between hacking coughs. I slammed the door, catching a glimpse of a second man inside and something big and black standing before him. That big and black thing was the source of the smoke. I inanely wondered why the smoke detectors didn't go off, but another part of me already guessed the answer: magic.

"Bill, what the hell is going on in there?" Sadie demanded, taking a step into the corridor as I walked out with the man. Bill was a little shorter than I, with pale skin and slicked-back dark hair.

He tried to cough a lung out on the carpet. I noticed that no one else was panicking. I took that as a sign that I shouldn't either, although it was hard to resist the impulse. I folded my arms across my chest and tried to blend in with the background, but I wanted to know what was going on, too.

Bill sucked some more air into his lungs, doubled over with his hands on his knees, before finally straightening. "Donovan is having a little bit of a disagreement with Aa-zal'min."

I wondered if it was in English, but Sadie seemed to understand. She began to rub her temples. From the office down the hall, there came another loud crash and someone shouting in a bizarre language.

"Are we going to lose another summoner?" Madison asked thoughtfully.

Summoner? I wondered but didn't ask. It didn't seem like the right time.

"The fact that he *can* summon Aa-zal'min is impressive," Sadie said with a heavy sigh. "Besides, he's our fourth summoner in less than a year. I can't bear the idea of moving onto a fifth. I'm just going to have to tell him—"

Whatever she was going to say was interrupted when the much talked of Donovan walked into the room. He was a tall man—taller than me—but spindly, with dark skin and pale eyes. "I'm sorry about that," he said. I thought he sounded sincere, though not embarrassed. "Aa-zal'min is back home now."

Sadie turned on him. "You can't be summoning demons from the Min-tarnan planes in the office. We don't have the proper wards."

Donovan gingerly touched the cuts on his cheek. "I know that now. I thought I had a strong enough warding circle, but the bastard broke out of it."

"They do that," Madison chimed in. "They'll only make the deal if they can't break your hold on them."

I finally couldn't hold back. "Can I ask a dumb question?"

Turning to me, Sadie smiled sympathetically. "What the hell are we talking about?"

"Basically."

"In the briefest explanation possible, some people can summon demons from other planes that have powers and abilities people here on earth don't. You can summon a demon and agree to a deal. Demons of all planes take contracts very seriously, but you have to understand their laws. Every deal is brokered by a lawyer well-versed in demonic law, which Bill— " She nodded to him. "—is. Donovan summons, and Bill does the contract work. Sometimes, however, a demon might be called up that is a little too strong for the location." Another dry look was cast at Donovan, who shrugged.

I scratched my head, thinking that was one hell of a thing. No pun intended.

Madison smiled at me. "Are you sure you still want to work here?"

Honestly, I couldn't say I was, but it was still the best—the only—option that I had.

CHAPTER TEN

After all the excitement died down and the other men had gone back to work, I filled out my forms. Sadie gave me a couple recommendations for butchers that stayed open all night (and doing incredible business since Cameron's Law) and I went home with just a quick stop at one of those shops. The guy at the counter was very understanding. I drank another jar as soon as I got home, but kept Sadie's warning in mind and restrained myself from binging.

Stanton wasn't one to dally, I could tell. I had my first job the next night. I didn't know much about it except I'd be going out with a woman named Sarah Beaumont, who was an animator. I also knew that an animator made a living creating short-lived zombies. I couldn't say I was looking forward to it.

Despite that, though, I felt a little better when I went home that night. The hunger had eased back to its dull roar after drinking the blood, and even if it wasn't the life I'd wanted, I had regained purpose. Something about this new job felt a little more important than previous jobs, and I had to admit I liked that. I wasn't sure if it would be enough, ultimately, but it was something. It was a place to start, and I would take what I could get.

When dawn came, I welcomed the oblivion, but it didn't feel quite so miserable.

❰○❱

After waking the next sunset, I showered, dressed, and had breakfast. Except for the hour and the blood, it was remarkably like any other day. I headed into the office at the expected time and waited in the front for Sarah Beaumont. Sadie and Madison were busy, so I kept to myself and read some outdated magazines. This included contemplating a theory that magazine companies only sent outdated issues to offices.

I didn't have too long to wait before a woman walked in. She was tall for a woman, though still several inches shorter than me, with short dark hair brushed away from an open face. I got to my feet. "Sarah Beaumont?"

"I take it you're my bodyguard?" She smiled.

"Apparently so."

"Come on, then." She waved for me to follow, tossing another wave back at Madison as she led me to her car. I couldn't help but think that I'd not had good luck getting into cars with women driving lately, but she was vouched for so I figured I'd have to be safe.

We drove in silence for a few minutes before I started talking. "Are we expecting specific trouble or just generally keeping an eye out? Sadie didn't get into a lot of the details."

She nodded, taking a right onto Sycamore Highway. "Both, really," she said. "I've had some LOHAV protestors show up at my jobs during the past couple of weeks. I presume you know the League of Humans Against Vampires? They're on the news often enough, after all." I nodded. "I don't know why they've chosen now. I also don't know if they know when my appointments are or have just been staking out graveyards. It's probably the latter, because other animators I know have had trouble too."

Sarah sighed heavily. "They haven't done anything violent," she continued, "but I don't trust that it will stay that way. They've got a long history of it. You must know what happened with Cameron St John, the werewolf who started the process for getting us all legal. LOHAV murdered him and nearly killed Sadie too, because she was with him. I don't know if you know it, but Madison is Cameron's sister. Cameron and Sadie were a couple, which is why Madison and Sadie are so close."

"I didn't know any of that," I said quietly. I just felt like more of a jerk now. "So, you think these protestors might get violent?"

"I wouldn't put it past them," she answered without hesitation. "One time, I had one of them get right in my face. I tripped and hit my head on a gravestone and almost lost control of my zombie. Not that it would have done anything but shamble around. They aren't like in the movies. A zombie will only attack someone if the animator tells it to, and we have limited range and time. It doesn't take long before they just fall back down dead. Still, it would not have been a nice sight.

"But I don't trust that they'll stick to shouting obscenities and being a nuisance, and I don't want to get hurt and don't want my clients getting hurt or even just frightened. I've already had a couple leave in the middle of appointments because they were so rattled by the protestors. A lot of the people I work with are grieving and in pain. They don't need a bunch of bigoted pigs getting in their face, so I asked Sadie if we could get someone to go out with me. She hired you."

Somehow, I felt humble as I said, "I'll do my best."

She flashed me a sidelong smile. "You just have to be a big wall of vampire."

It sounded like something I could handle.

We arrived at the graveyard and met Sarah's client, who turned out to be a young woman. I doubted she was old enough to legally buy a drink, but she'd been legal to get married. It was her husband in the grave. He'd been a soldier in the Middle East, but they'd been able to ship a mostly-complete corpse back. She hadn't wanted him buried anywhere but next to his parents, so here he was.

"I just want to say good-bye," she said to Sarah, sniffling. I lingered on the outside, watching. "My mother said I shouldn't. That I should keep my farewells to the funeral, and I did, but...I can't go on without having that chance to actually speak to him again. They say you can do that, right? That if it's close enough to his death, they can talk like they did?"

"In a limited capacity, yes," Sarah assured her with a small smile. "It's always harder to handle than you imagine. I'll warn you now. But you can say good-bye and tell him that you love him. And he can say it back."

The woman inhaled deeply and nodded.

I felt like an intruder on something private, so I tried to stay back. I watched Sarah move to the open grave. She opened the coffin, reaching down and doing something I couldn't see. There was no chanting or burning candles or magic dust. She just reached down, and magic prickled the air. I felt it all along my arms and in my hair.

A hand reached up and pulled a body out of the grave behind it. He wasn't as badly decomposed as I expected, though still gross. The woman bore the sight of him remarkably well, but thank God, she didn't kiss him. She almost looked like she would, and I didn't think I could have handled that.

"Oh, Joshua, I've missed you so much," she said with a sob breaking her words in half.

"I'm sorry I left you," he replied, slurring only a little. "I won't be able to take care of you now, like I promised."

She covered her mouth with her hands, sobbing again. "I couldn't let you go without having one more moment to say I loved you. And I'm going to miss you so much."

He was in the dress uniform of a Marine. He reached out, like he was going to touch her, but stopped. "I wish I didn't have to leave again. I love you."

A car door shutting behind me drew my attention away from the creepy, yet heartbreaking, scene. I saw an angry face storming toward us and moved quickly to intercept.

"This is private business." I didn't have to dig too deep to sound authoritative.

"Get out of my way." The woman tried to push past me, but I made a decently solid presence right in her way. She huffed. "They have no right to be here doing this!"

"What *right* do you have to say so?" Maybe I would have agreed before, but before, I never would have actually seen it. Never have seen the look in the widow's eyes when her husband spoke to her, if just for one moment more. I'll never forget that look, and those eyes were like nails in my feet, keeping me there, keeping this woman from getting by and ruining that moment.

"It's unnatural. It's against the law of nature." She stared up into my face.

"Well, I think it's unnatural to have a big ole bigot stick up the ass, but you seem to be managing it." My faded accent got stronger when I said that for some reason. Should I have said it? Probably not. It wasn't very professional, but I really couldn't make myself give a damn. Her wide-eyed gasp pleased me. "Why don't you take your sorry self and be moving along?" I suggested with a mean smile and a flash of the new fangs. "We don't need your kind here, and I'm going to stand in your way until they're done if you don't go. I might even pick you up and carry you to your car. This is private business."

Something in my face—I think it was the teeth—sent her scrambling with an indignant squawk.

Turning back, I watched the soldier climb back into his

grave. The widow kneeled at the edge, staying as close to her husband as she could for as long as she could until he was asleep again and Sarah closed the coffin. The young woman still cried, but she smiled too and thanked the animator profusely. Sarah put a hand on her shoulder, and we stayed there until she stopped crying and was able to go home.

Chapter Eleven

We drove back to the office in silence.

Something was bothering me, but the primary source of it took me a while to figure out. To the obvious, the bother would have been what I had just witnessed. Before, it would have been disconcerting enough just to witness the animation, but the emotion of it would have been worse for me. I had never been comfortable with shows of emotion, other than anger, because I never knew what to do with myself. I always kept my own bottled up inside, because I had been taught from a young age to keep them in check.

Now, it was easy to accept the reanimation of the deceased, and that bothered me more than the emotive display. I had never been much of a fan of anything preternatural, despite my tendency to gravitate toward the imitative crowd. But I had never had the blind hatred that drove a person to all but assault people in a private moment like the one we now drove away from. I couldn't help but think of the news. I had seen stories about protests of things other people thought were unnatural. I had thought those protests were heinous, but I'd never applied it to something like this...until now.

The blind bias of my previous life embarrassed me.

And yet, that wasn't all of what rankled in my mind. There was something else, and it had a more immediate feeling to it. It connected somehow to the restlessness I always felt. Something the soldier had said had caught onto it, or something related to it, and it stuck.

Sarah and I parted ways at the office. I did my best to smile politely and say good night without appearing as distracted as I was, but when something bothered me like this, I was compelled to dig deep into my mind to figure it out.

It didn't take me long, and in a way, I wasn't surprised. It was Cielle. I couldn't easily define why, but my rage had begun to dissolve when I thought of her. Maybe it had been the crawling out of my apartment and into the light—figuratively speaking—that made me start to look at all sides. Don't mistake me, I was still furious for the whole murder and turning, but I did begin to wonder about her reasons. I thought about the things she had said as I was storming out of the bar, and again at my apartment.

Cielle had turned me for a reason, and while that might not have justified her actions, I began to feel a need to know what that reason was. Maybe it would help, and maybe it would ease the dark spots in my mind. Now that I was starting to put pieces of a new life together, the shadows stood out more than before. I wanted to be done with them.

So I turned off the path to home, turned the car around, and started driving a route quickly becoming far too familiar. I drove to 5. It was, after all, where I had found her before, and I didn't have anywhere else to try. How she had found my apartment was a question worth asking, since we had never exchanged addresses or phone numbers, only body fluids.

Walking into the bar as a fang was a much different experience. I could see everything much more clearly. Since I wasn't on a rampaging exit this time, I actually paid attention to what I saw. I kind of wished I hadn't. I'll spare you the details, but fangs are nuts. We'll leave it at that.

Quintus was behind the bar. I wondered if he lived there. I dimly recalled tearing apart a bedroom before storming downstairs and out of the bar the night I was turned.

With my new night vision, I could see him better too. He was still huge, still dark, but now I saw the rugged face and the faint history of scars. I wondered about them but wasn't about to ask. He eyed me, curious but otherwise impassive.

"I didn't expect to see you again." He set a glass down in front of me. "Can I get you a drink?"

"Sure." I tried not to fidget on the stool under his unwavering gaze. "I came looking for Cielle."

He turned that gaze to the blood he poured into the glass and didn't look up again. Something about his face looked pensive, though he seemed to be a man with many years of practice at keeping an impassive expression. He didn't say a word, instead capping the bottle, taking up the glass, and walking down the bar with both.

"Well? Have you seen her?" I asked louder, getting off the stool and following.

He looked back at me once, sweeping his gaze over the patrons as if weighing them. "Come on. I want to show you something."

I was getting very tired very quickly of the mystery shit. Just because you lived forever didn't mean everything had to be hooded secrets and hushed tones.

I made a mental note to remember that.

I followed the mass of a once-living man to the back, to the same damnable room that had caused so many of my problems. It must have been his office by the easy way he moved about it. I shut the door behind me, planning on raising my voice.

"I'm getting real tired of this stalking and shushing shit being all a fang has to offer," I growled. "Have you seen Cielle or not?"

Quintus pinned me with a stare, and it was a damn scary one. I'm a big guy, but Quintus is bigger, and the look on his face told me all I needed to know about who would win in an alleyway brawl. I shut my trap and looked apologetic.

He kept his gaze on me a moment longer before he looked away in agitation. "I'm sorry to have to tell you this, but Cielle is dead." He took a long gulp from the glass in his hand and sat down. "I mean, for good."

I stared at him and felt an icy hand clutch my spine. "Are you serious?"

Leaning back in his chair, he crossed his arms across his chest and finally looked at me again. "Yes, I'm afraid so." I couldn't read much from his expression until I saw his big shoulders rise and fall with a heavy sigh. "I saw it happen."

"The fuck, you saw it? And you didn't, I don't know, throw that big fucking hunk of body in there and try to stop it?" My hackles rose, and that white-hot rage I'd been battling since this whole whirlwind began came back in a storm.

"She was very upset after what happened between you two," he replied, his tone level and patient. "I have always counseled her that engaging in acts such as what brought you under her spell was unwise, but she was ever of her own mind about things." He paused thoughtfully. "She was always so convinced that she could encourage her way out of a difficult situation, but she had not counted on you in the least." Quintus smiled faintly, but there was no mirth to it. "She went out, saying she was looking to speak with you again, and I expected her back by dawn. As dawn approached, she had not yet returned; she kept a room here instead of the Coven House. I was about to turn in, giving her up for having found you and brought you around to her way of thinking.

"I heard a commotion from the parking lot. All of my patrons had already long departed back to their safe places for the day. Errantly, I went out, as my age has given me some prolonged strength against the dead sleep in those early gray hours. It was then I saw her outside, engaged in an argument with someone. It was another vampire, though the light and the distance prevented me from recognizing who it might be.

I could only tell it was a man and he was a vampire. They began to fight in earnest. I wanted to help her, but I felt dawn pressing hard. I was amazed that they could still move as much as they did.

"Even so, I was just about to get out of the door to help when he..." He paused, and I saw the first flash of strong emotion in his eyes as he cleared his throat. "He cut off her head. It was horrible to see. He fled after that, and I still would have gone out to her but for first rays of sun coming over the horizon. I succumbed to the dead sleep there in the corridor. It was luck or damned fortune that I remained out of the sunlight and was not myself taken under."

He stopped talking and broke the mesmerized hold he'd had over me while relating the story. I took up the unfinished glass of blood still on the desk, not even thinking before I took a long drink and gave myself a moment to think. It didn't help. I couldn't process it. Guilt warred with rage. The former was fresher, but the latter was deeper. The two were violent in the mind and permitted few other thoughts between them.

"What happened to her?" I asked, in barely half a voice.

"When I awoke at dusk, I went out to her. She was not in the...best of shape." He shook his head and poured a second glass, drinking it himself. "Despite what the entertainment industry would have you believe, we do not turn to dust. However, if we are left in the sun, we do char. I contacted the authorities, but as I feared, there was not much that could be done after so much time having passed. The cause of death was quite obvious. There was no evidence. I think they considered me, briefly, but given my circumstances, they rightfully dismissed that thought."

Her beautiful face flashed through my mind. I heard her pleading with me to stay, telling me that it was a matter of life and death. I guess she'd been right.

"They are trying to find her family, but she never

spoke to me of her past. I informed them that I would take responsibility for her remains if no one stepped forward to claim her. They will keep looking, though there isn't much to go on."

"She knew someone was after her." I stared into the dark red. It wasn't talking. "What I don't understand is… why me?" Tearing my gaze away, I looked up at him, utterly dumbfounded. "What did she want with me?"

Quintus shook his head. "That was something I believe was between you and her. She did not tell me what, if anything, was after her. Cielle only said she was worried and needed help, but she needed something special. By the manner in which she kept after you, you apparently had it. I vaguely remember her words regarding you as being 'a remarkable human being.' She seemed to think you would be just what she needed."

For the life of me, I couldn't figure out what she could have seen in me. I doubted she saw in me what Sadie had hired me for. This sounded much worse than that, and far more complicated.

Suddenly, I felt a hundred bricks between my shoulder blades. I slumped into the chair opposite him with my hand wrapped around the glass. Quintus refilled it without my asking.

What was I supposed to do with this now? I couldn't stop being mad at her, even now that she was dead. She'd killed me, used me, but she was dead. She'd needed my help and had taken some extreme measures to try to secure it. I'd left her behind, and there seemed to be no escape from the simple fact that she was dead because of it.

I might as well have killed her myself.

Chapter Twelve

I spent the rest of the night wallowing at 5. Quintus was very patient with me, but he did kick me out in time to get home before dawn. I thought mostly about Cielle, and myself, and the mysterious man who had killed her. My mind was very confused when I fell into my daylight sleep.

It wasn't any better when I woke the next night. I didn't want to go down to the office. I'm not too proud to admit I would rather have reverted to sulking like after the last time I'd been at that damned bar. That place was bad for my health.

Still, I didn't need to fuck up a second job. I didn't have an appointment with Beaumont, but I had promised to do some work on the computers. After breakfast, I headed to the office and got to work.

"Are you almost done?" Madison sat on the edge of her desk, peering over her shoulder at me after I'd been there about a half-hour. "A secretary without her computer is only half-busy."

"You work too much, Madison." I glanced up from behind her monitor with a half-hearted smirk. "Don't you ever do anything fun? I know I haven't been here long, but you seem like you're here all the time." I couldn't explain the easy feeling I had around her. She felt like everyone's little sister.

She glanced back at me again, sticking her tongue out. "I already have Sadie on my case about that. I don't need you helping her. She hijacked my life to send me to New York for a weekend and even there, I couldn't get away from working. She learned her lesson."

I typed commands and clicked on things. It was so familiar that I barely remember what I did. I'm not even sure I paid much attention while I was doing it. My mind kept trying to return to Cielle and that little bundle of confusion, but I resisted and tried to not be a miserable person for Madison to be around. I liked her too much. "Come on. You're young. You're beautiful. You have a working pulse. You can't want to be here all the time."

The werewolf, as I had learned her to be, laughed. "This is what I get for working around too many vampires. I get my pulse used against me."

"It was a compliment."

"Thank you."

"You're welcome."

I worked for a little while longer and then declared it all done.

She grinned. "Finally!" She came around and took the seat, barely waiting for me to get out of it first. Even in my state, I wouldn't have argued if she'd wanted to sit on my lap, but I knew there would never be anything romantic between us. I had way too much bullshit baggage to deal with, and she felt like a sister.

"The whole office isn't filled with vampires, you know." I'm not sure why I felt compelled to point this out, but I did. Maybe I just needed to fill the void with talk, lest my mind do it for me.

"No one else seems to spend any time in the office, though, but the two of you," she pointed out while typing, not even looking at me. Had it been so obnoxious when I was doing it five minutes before? "I mean, Dakota rarely comes in here, and Beaumont spends most of her nights in the graveyards, as you're learning."

"What about the new guy?" I leaned back against the desk, folding my arms. "So far, all I know about him is that he nearly loosed a demon of destruction on us."

Madison shook her head. "It's too soon to tell if he'll last, especially after that little display, but he's not a vampire. You don't see animators or summoners that are." She stopped typing and frowned thoughtfully. "I'm not really sure why that is. Maybe the turning takes the power out of them. It would be weird for an animator to be a vampire."

The terminology took getting used to. I understood some of what she said, but not all of it. "Why would it be weird? Seems like a far-fetched enough idea to work. Mystical powers and what-have-you." I wiggled my fingers at her spookily. She wasn't impressed, if she had even noticed.

"Well, you guys are technically dead. A really, really strong animator—like, one of the verge of powering up to a necromancer, or an actual necromancer—can control you like they do the corpses they raise." She smiled apologetically, like she didn't want to be the messenger of that little bombshell.

I grimaced. "That's a disturbing thought. Is Sarah strong enough to do that? No one has said anything about her being a necromancer."

She shrugged. "I couldn't tell you for sure, because it's never come up. She might, but she's also one the most ethical animators I've ever met. I wouldn't fear her."

I wasn't sure if that sounded comforting or not, but I did feel a little better, since I had met Sarah. She seemed like a kind woman, so no, I didn't feel like I should fear her. Still, as if I didn't have enough weight on my mind, the thought there was a type of power out there that could control me like a puppet was worrisome.

"How common is that kind of power?" I had to ask.

"Not very, I promise." Madison offered a warm smile.

The front door slammed open and bounced against the wall. Two tall, robust shifters stormed in.

"I don't want to hear it out of you!" the woman shouted, waving a hand at the man behind her without looking at him. "Just because you spent a century chilling out with some crazy supernatural monks in Asian mountains doesn't mean I want to hear one word out of your mouth about meditation or finding my chi or calming down."

"You don't scare me," the man declared, crossing his arms over his chest. "You can pull your scary hunter routine with the rest of the world, but don't forget, Anneliese, I know you."

"Don't call me that here!" she snapped, whirling on him.

I just stared. Madison did briefly as well before she waded in. "Hey!" They ignored her, their argument continuing. "*Hey*!" It still didn't work. She then made another noise that sounded a lot like a bark and for some reason, that got their attention. "I know that you two still have a few centuries of sibling rivalry to catch up on, but be nice. We have a new friend. D, this is Dakota. She's our hunter. This is her brother Edward, who is... I don't know. Are you helping or just running around after her to piss her off?"

"Helping."

"Pissing me off."

Madison sighed. "Well, knock it off. You're giving me a headache. What is going on?"

"Nosy Nellie here has an issue with how I do my job, despite the fact that he wasn't invited in the first place," Dakota snapped.

"I just wanted to help. She's reckless." Edward looked at her dryly. "And my only problem is that I don't think it was necessary to scare small children."

I had heard briefly about Dakota from Sadie while filling out my employment forms. She was over four hundred years old and a shifter unlike any other. She was a lot more powerful than most shifters. Having two of them in a knock-down, drag-out shouting match in the front office was more than a little concerning. They were both my height and weight too, so there was little advantage to me if things became a real brawl.

"It's not my fault that kid happened to be walking past when I shifted," she muttered, folding her arms over her chest. "It wasn't like I jumped on him or anything. He just saw me shift and freaked out. That's not *my* fault."

"I'm never going to have to work with either of them, am I?" I asked Madison, leaning back toward her.

She smiled. "It's not likely. Even so, they're both a lot of bluster."

I wasn't so sure of that, but I didn't say anything as they went off down the corridor, still arguing.

Chapter Thirteen

I was just on my way out when Sadie came in. She had a broad, dark-haired man following her, and my super senses caught the scent of cat about him the way I caught the scent of dog around Madison. It was subtle and not unpleasant, but gave me a clear indication of species.

"D," Sadie said with a polite smile of greeting. "Vance, this is our newest employee I told you about. D, this is my boyfriend, Detective Vance Johnston."

He gave me the once-over with his near-amber eyes, like he was assessing whether I was going to make trouble for his girl. I still felt too sorry for myself to present much of a threat, so I stood and let him examine me. Apparently, I wasn't judged a nuisance. He smiled and offered his hand, which I shook.

"I was just on my way out," I said to both. "Good meeting you, Detective. I will see you later, Sadie." I'd had about as much socialization as I could stand for one evening, so I nodded and left.

My mind wasn't in a great place, and I didn't feel like being chatty with a police detective; especially when someone semi-close to me had recently been murdered. I didn't care if it made me seem suspicious or what, that social disturbia that came with being nervous around police was enough to drive me out of the office. I couldn't get caught at anything if I was out of sight, right?

I was nearly to my car when I heard it: the scuffing of a

shoe against cement. I don't know why that sound clicked in my head, but it did. I spun around just in time to see a man fly at me. I'd never been very good at staying out of fights when I was younger, and the teenage instincts were still in a modest state. Dodging to the side just in time to let him slam into my car door, I got out half my sentiment with a "what the" and then the rest was lost to the need to move.

Spinning to face him, I met his eyes. He was out for blood. It didn't matter if I knew who he was, he was intent on coming after me. This wasn't a case of mistaken identity. He must have had me in mind before I walked out of the building.

It's funny the thoughts that come to you from one second to the other.

He was damn fast—too fast. Unnaturally fast. His right hand hooked around at my face with preternatural speed, and I barely threw myself back a step, letting his fist fly by just an inch from my nose.

Now, I've never been much of a trained fighter, but I've had a few scuffles in my time and having a fucking fang come at me from out of nowhere ignited all my senses of self-preservation. I hissed through my fangs and felt something dark and angry surge through my veins where blood used to flow.

He took another swing, and I caught his fist in my hand. He was more surprised than I, losing the snarl on his face for just a moment. I didn't have time for this shit, so I hauled him forward and off balance. His shoulder popped. Momma always said I had a hard head. While his pasty face came at me, I slammed my forehead into his. Unnatural adrenaline surged through me so hard I didn't even feel the pain, taking pleasure in watching him reel back.

He thought I'd be easy to take down, whatever his reasons were. He had no fucking idea the shit I'd been through, but he was about to learn why now was possibly the worst time to fuck with me.

He stumbled, and I lunged. He was a few inches shorter than me and scrawny. I put all my weight and height into the downward punch that cracked his undead nose. Gravity drew normally stagnant blood down, and the scent enflamed whatever senses remained silent until then. It blinded me for a moment as I grabbed his short hair and pulled him toward me, sinking my fangs into the muscle of his shoulder.

Jerking away with a girly scream, he left some of his flesh in my mouth and bolted for the trees. Honest to God, I was about to break down on all fours and tear after his ass. I had a taste, a piece of something hell bent to work me over. I didn't want to back down. I wanted to take it head-on and tear it apart. The yawning pit in my soul had opened up, and all that rage poured out.

The office door banged open with a ruckus loud enough to break my rage-sickened reverie for a flash of a moment. Sadie and Vance rushed out, the detective with a gun in his hand and Sadie smelling the air. "D, are you okay?" she asked right away. I knew she'd be able to smell the blood.

I took reflexive deep breaths. Funny thing, that. The floodgates slammed shut, and the gaping rage evaporated. I spat the blood and gore from the fucker's shoulder onto the pavement. "Yeah." My voice sounded flat in my ears. "Some crazy fuck just came after me." I could have been telling them it was going to rain. Turning my head, I met Vance's look and could tell the Cop was coming out. "Fuck knows who he is or what he wants. Never seen him before. He was a fang like me, though, that I know. Bastard ran off when he realized I wasn't so easy to put down."

"You should come to the station and fill out a report," Vance advised, holstering his weapon. "And we should get some of the blood from your mouth, run it against our database."

That dark something was still inside. I laughed without

humor. "Now there's something you don't hear every day."

He smiled, but with no more mirth than me. "It's more common these days, I think."

"I suppose it is at that." I paused. "What about the stuff I spit out instead?"

"Easier to not have dirt in it. Your mouth doesn't make saliva anymore, so what's in your mouth now—surprisingly—is likely to be less contaminated."

Lovely. Well. So much for the wallowing.

I went down to the station with him and didn't clean the blood off until after I'd gotten there and they'd taken their sample. I felt kind of like a freak, even in Adelheid, walking around with blood dried on my chin and neck. Vampire blood does not taste like living blood, either. It's bad. It's kind of like a muted version of something crawling in your mouth and dying.

I'd tell you about filling out the report, but I barely remember. Everything felt mechanical to me, because I was too deep in my mind. I was angry and confused, but with nowhere to take it. The world seemed shaded with the darkness I felt within.

Who the hell had that guy been, and why come after me? He'd had murder in his eyes. I'd seen it clear as I've seen anything. A few weeks ago, I would have thought I'd be able to tell if there was someone out there who wanted to kill me. Now, I was learning from painful experience that I knew jack shit about it, which was about as much as I was able to put in the report. At least they let me take a minute to clean myself up as best I could.

Once they were done with me, I left the station and just started walking. I didn't have any destination in mind, but I needed to move. I couldn't stay still like this. It had taken all my will power to remain in the seat with the police. Without that strong motivation, I couldn't do it now.

My muscles twitched with agitation. After walking for a few minutes, I knew this wasn't going to do it. I needed to do something more, but I couldn't think of what. I hadn't lived the most active of lives when I'd been amongst the living, so I wasn't familiar with this feeling and didn't really have any ideas of what to do with it.

I wanted to hit someone, something, anything. I'd gotten all revved up for a fight and when it ended so abruptly, I think I still had some of it left. I was looking for a fight, which was why my subconscious prodded me toward some of the less reputable parts of town.

These were areas I had been to before but generally kept my visits brief. Being something of a classic small New England town, there wasn't any *really* bad area, like with drive-bys and dead bodies on doorsteps every morning with the paper, but there were some shadier than others. A place where you could go and no one was likely to remember your being there.

In the mood I was in, I seemed to navigate instinctively toward these places, and I can say one thing for certain: if I had gone there looking for trouble, I found it.

Chapter Fourteen

I walked down the sidewalk, hands stuffed in pockets and head down. I heard a muffled scream. Fuck this vampire hearing. My nerves were raw, and this was not where I needed to be. I wasn't afraid. I was looking for blood on my own. If I'd been human, I wouldn't be feeling this. 'If I'd been human' was the whole problem. If I were human, I would have gone running the other way, telling myself it was some wild animal or an alley cat with its latest victim.

I wouldn't have let it bother me if I were human. I never would have followed the sound to the shadowed alley.

I never would have found the two men and the girl.

The metallic tang of blood on the air heightened my senses as soon as I came near. It hammered me when I came around the corner. The voices were male.

"Keep her fucking mouth shut," one hissed at the other.

Naked depravity was something the media and entertainment industry assaulted us with, reminding us of it, bashing us over the head with it so that we would do something about it. Give to charity. Keep a light on and watch like hawks through our window blinds for shady characters shuffling around in the bushes. Worse, it hardened us to it. It made us used to it. It was the way the world was.

She was a pale thing and didn't have any fight in her. The one with his back to me was dropping his pants, baring himself for the cowardly act. He was a man, and he had terrible things in mind. His partner in the act licked his lips with eagerness, with either the forbidden thrill of voyeurism or the impatience of his 'turn.'

Fuck this.

Rage was becoming a fast friend of mine. I felt it bubble up and wrap around me like a lover's embrace, tighter and stronger than Cielle's grip on my life as she threw it into chaos. It all boiled up in an instant, exploding me to action. It was that untamable, undeniable force of punishment that set itself squarely in my mind.

I lunged forward with unholy speed, recklessly knocking aside the one with his pants down and sending him flying into the other. They fell in a tangle of limbs and curses. I wanted to check on the girl, but that would come in a minute. I wanted to play with these two.

There was so much blood, and I hadn't even begun yet. The alleyway was filled with the copper tang, and the sound of her heartbeat was dimming. Each faint thump fed the fire in my mind.

The two men hadn't found their feet before I was on them. I grabbed a fistful of shirt in each hand, bellowing as I flung them into the walls like I was slinging dirty laundry. A nose crunched and that bastard slumped in a heap while the second managed to stand. This had been the Other One. He had a cut to his brow, dripping blood in his eye.

I saw the blood and smiled, fangs out. He blanched, pissing himself and praying his mother had never rode his father raw. I lunged into him like a running back through a defensive line, head and shoulder down and straight into center mass. All the air in his body rushed out in a great gush as he smacked against the wall. Straightening briefly, I grabbed his face and rammed my fist into it for all it was worth.

He fell into a pile beside his buddy.

I wanted to do more, but I heard the girl moan. It was

faint, and her heartbeat reined in my urge to do more to these two piles of scum.

She looked about twenty. Her blonde hair shone until it reached her shoulders, where it matted with blood to her skin and clothes from the long gash across the front of her neck. Her eyes were open, gray in color but with the life fast fading from them.

"Oh, God, please don't die." I didn't know this woman, but it was suddenly the most important thing in my world that she didn't die.

I looked at her neck and considered putting my hand over the wound, to stop the blood, but knew it would be useless. She had lost too much. Briefly, her eyes met mine, but I couldn't tell if she actually saw me before they drifted upward, losing focus.

For a moment, the length of a heartbeat, I sat frozen.

I had to do something.

Some instinct or idea too deep to recognize consciously took control of me. It was so strong I almost disassociated. I was almost outside of my body, watching my own actions.

I picked her frail body up in my arms and found a fortuitous abandoned warehouse nearby. I managed, again only by good fortune, to get into the building without anyone seeing me. I know that only because no cops showed up to arrest me for being the one who hurt her.

Finding a nice dark corner, I laid her carefully on the dusty floor. I almost apologized for it being such a mess, but I knew she was unaware. There was still the faintest of heartbeats, but it slowed more by the moment.

"I'm not entirely sure how this works, but I hope it does." I whispered it. I'm not sure why. No one else was there. Who was I worried would hear?

I didn't know what parts of this were required, so I did everything I remembered.

Her neck was mangled, so I brought her wrist to my mouth and sunk my fangs in, again resisting the urge to apologize. So much blood had been lost that I had to work hard to drink any of it, but I didn't take much. I then bit my own wrist, tearing open some skin before pressing it to her lips. I didn't hear her swallow but imagined some made it down her throat.

The one thing I didn't do was kill her, because I knew she was already there.

I watched instead. A few steps away, I sat with my legs bent. I felt like a terrified child, just barely keeping myself from hugging my knees to my chest. Her heart slowed to the point where each beat surprised me, and her breathing became so shallow that even I strained to hear it until it all stopped.

What was supposed to happen now? I tried to peer through the blood haze in my memories to remember how it went for me. Cielle had killed me one night, but I didn't awake in my new state until the next. I supposed that meant I wouldn't know if it had worked until tomorrow night.

I'd have to wait.

That didn't bode well for me. I wouldn't leave her alone, but staying here until dawn meant I had time to think. I also worried about what would happen during the daylight hours when I had no control, but could I risk trying to take her somewhere else?

I tried to process questions one at a time, or my brain threatened to overload. My mental motherboard was going to fry any second.

I didn't see how I could risk moving her. I had walked here, which meant I'd have to walk with a dead girl in my arms for a long time. It just couldn't go well, and I didn't want to do anything to interrupt what might be happening in her. I couldn't make it worse, but I could possibly stop it from getting better.

I checked my cell phone and saw that it was a lot later than I had thought, so dawn wasn't far off. I couldn't risk getting caught out in it, but at least I wouldn't have that long to wait before unconsciousness took me. Being out of my own control and not in a safe place was frightening, but at least it would all be out of my control and I wouldn't have to worry about fucking something up.

It was a good-thing/bad-thing kind of deal.

What the hell was I doing?

There was still time enough before oblivion to worry about that, and I had no answer, because I had no clue. The next question and answer, though, ended up with: what else could I do? I couldn't let her die when I had the power to help her, right? I mean, I knew I could be a bastard, but I wasn't immoral or heartless.

I had to do something.

Now, I just had to hope it was the right thing and might actually do some good. I hoped she wouldn't wake up and hate me with the same bloodlust I'd turned on Cielle, but I hadn't been the one to kill her. There was hope.

There *was* hope, right?

I picked her up again, feeling an ache in my chest at the thought of this not working. I stamped it down, shuffling deeper into the abandoned building where there were no windows. I found a storage room with some old empty crates. I settled myself down in a corner and didn't let her go. I tried to make her dead form as comfortable as I could, as if that would be some consolation for her when she woke up... like me.

I just had to cross my fingers and hope, hope that everything would be okay, and hope as the coming day stole my consciousness that we would both wake up the next night, and everything would be...okay.

Chapter Fifteen

I woke with the following sunset and was immediately relieved I had, that nothing terrible had befallen my incapacitated self while I slept away the daylight in this abandoned storeroom.

My next thought turned to the girl. I'd been holding onto her like a teddy bear before I fell asleep, but she damn well wasn't there now. I sat up fast and nearly hopped right out of my skin to find her already sitting up, just staring at me.

"Jumpin' Jesus on a pogo stick!" I shouted foggily. The suddenness and her unblinking eyes made my brain revert to the good ol' boy days.

"What's happened to me?" she asked. Her voice was rough. She seemed confused and uncertain, but not terrified or angry. I had been expecting terrified or angry. Confused, okay. Uncertain, okay. But the semi-calm way she asked it… That was unnerving.

"I found you last night," I managed after a minute to get my bearings. No sense lying. Lies have a way of coming back to bite you on the ass. Look at how I'd ended up here. "I…came up on some guys on you in the alley. They cut your throat, and…I did the only thing I could think of." I hesitated but forced myself to go on. "I'm a vampire. So, I bit you, gave you some of my blood, and tried to make sure you survived. One way or another."

She tilted her head. Sections of blood-matted blonde

hair fell away from her neck, and her pale brows drew together. "I'm a vampire?"

I nodded, looking down at my hands. Seeing blood on them, I rubbed them against my jeans to try to clean it off. "Yeah, and I'm sorry. I couldn't think of anything else to do. There was no time to get you to a hospital where it would do you any good, and the daylight was coming fast, and—"

I lifted my head to look at her and stopped yammering. I watched her touch her throat. Dried blood rubbed off, but the skin beneath was healed over as if nothing had happened. She stared at her fingertips and frowned. "I remember being dragged off the street, but I don't remember much else."

"I wish I could have gotten there sooner. I could have stopped them before they got started. If I hadn't been so damn angry, I—"

Something about her made me uncertain. I didn't usually stammer, but her presence brought out something almost bashful in me and kept me from being embarrassed about it.

"It's all right." Her voice was distant but sincere. "I'm alive, in a fashion, and I'm sure that's more than I could have said if you hadn't shown up at all."

I shut up for a minute then. I had trouble believing she wasn't angry about all this. I guess because of the way it happened for me, I thought everyone was angry about being turned, but she seemed genuinely okay, all things considered. She was certainly handling things a lot better than I had.

"We should probably call the cops and, uh, report what happened to you."

Something hard flashed through her eyes. "No," she said and then smiled faintly, shaking her head. "There's no reason. I don't know who the men were and barely remember it. I'm alive and whole, and if anyone should try anything again, I imagine I'll be in a better position to defend myself. I don't want to deal with cops."

Her reaction bothered me. "You're not on the run from something, are you?"

"No." She shook her head with a faint laugh. I had a lot of trouble imagining her as any kind of criminal. Maybe a jaywalker. "It's just that cops can be so...overwhelming and kind of pushy. I don't want the trouble when there really isn't much they can do. A report from me would say very little."

"Uh, all right. If you say so." I still wasn't entirely convinced, but I believed her. It was an odd contradiction, but since I typically didn't care for a lot of trouble, I couldn't say I didn't understand. I might not have reported that attack outside the office had Sadie's cop boyfriend not been there. "So, do you have a name?"

Appearing relieved I wasn't going to pressure her, she smiled softly. "I'm Cassandra. And you are?"

I blurted my full name out before I could stop myself. Why did I want her to know? I hated when people used it, so I did my damnedest not to let anybody know it. Only my mother could get away with it, but for some reason, I wanted Cassandra to know. "Most people call me D." My ego felt compelled to add that.

"I've always just been Cassandra."

Another long moment of silence passed between us. What the hell did a person talk about at a time like this? She had blood all over her, and I had some too. I was trying to figure out what the Welcome to Vampirism handbook said when I still hadn't read the whole thing.

It was awkward.

"I can take you home," I suggested. "I mean, you can't want to stay here in this warehouse, obviously, so I can make—"

She cut me off, shaking her head. "No, I don't need to go home. I don't want to go home. I was leaving home when I ended up in that alley."

I began to feel like a car that kept revving the engine only to be brought to a screeching halt. Call the cops? No. Go home? No. Okay, what did that leave me, other than the obvious three-for-three conclusion that just because a woman had been turned, it didn't make her any less confusing.

"Well, then, I will take you wherever you want to go or wherever you were headed," I tried the next likely path and crossed my fingers.

"I didn't really have a plan." She shrugged sheepishly. "You don't have to worry about me. I'll figure my way out."

Memories of Sadie's 'blood fever' warnings came ringing back clear in my mind, and I shook my head fervently. "Oh no, no new vampires allowed on their own in the first few days. I've heard the horror stories, and I am not going to be responsible for that."

Large, gray eyes blinked at me, but then she nodded. "All right, I can accept that. I guess I wasn't really thinking about the vampire thing."

"It takes some getting used to," I agreed. It left me in something of a quandary, though, because if she didn't want to go home and didn't have anywhere else, then what was I supposed to do with her?

My head hurt. I wish being a vampire saved you from stress and tension headaches, but it doesn't.

"I suppose you could stay with me, but I realize you don't know me from Adam..." I trailed off, feeling a little helpless and bereft of options.

"If you're responsible for me and my new state of being, then I suppose it's really the only option." She didn't look bothered by the idea.

Of course, now that she had said that, I realized she was entirely right. I couldn't have taken her home and left her there, or anywhere else, as she was. She needed someone to help her through the transition, although she already looked like she had a better grip on things than I did.

I was her sire, which just sounded fucking *weird* to me.

"Okay then," I said, "I guess it looks like we're going back to my place. It's not much, but it'll keep us out of the sun." I looked her over for a moment and then pulled my T-shirt off. I still had an A-shirt on under it. "Here." I gave it to her. "Walking around covered in blood just won't do, Cameron's Law or not."

She smiled gratefully, and I turned around to let her change. Cassandra tapped me on the shoulder a few moments later. My shirt hung almost like a dress on her, but I had to admit she was pretty cute. That thought got cut off fast.

"Let's get back to the apartment and see about vampire one-oh-one," I said as we left the warehouse.

Chapter Sixteen

W e got back to my apartment without running into any problems. The last thing either of us needed was a cop, or even so much as a pedestrian, stopping us and asking, "Hey, where'd all that blood come from?" What do you say to that? "Snack gone wrong?" I'd end up on the six o'clock news.

Once inside my place, I let out a breath of relief. "Have a seat. Make yourself comfortable." I went into the kitchen and got two jars of blood. I hoped she wouldn't have the same aversion to it I did, because I knew the hunger sucked. I walked into the living room and found her with her legs folded under her on the sofa. She looked remarkably at ease, all things considered.

"Blood?" she asked, looking at the jars in my hand.

I smiled apologetically. "Yeah, it's unavoidable. You're on a liquid diet from here on. I know it seems pretty gross, but we're made for it."

She took the jar without hesitation and pulled off the top. After one sniff, she took an experimental sip and then downed the rest. Using the tip of her tongue, she cleaned a bit from the corner of her mouth.

I found it inappropriately hot and cleared my throat before drinking my own jar, way too fast, to get my mind off it.

I was entirely out of my element. My brain jumped to the first place it had jumped before, when I needed fang-related help. I excused myself and stepped into the bedroom, fishing my cell phone out of my pocket to call the office. I kept my chatter with Madison short, and she transferred me to Sadie.

"What's up, D? I thought you didn't have an appointment till later. Is everything okay?" She really was a nice person. I still wished I hadn't been such a dick to her at Phoenix.

"I have a vampire in my apartment."

She paused, like she was waiting for the punch line. "What's so odd about that? I doubt your membership has been revoked."

I wish I could have laughed. "I have a vampire in my apartment that I turned."

There was a long pause. "You *what*?"

"I turned her."

"This isn't a joke?"

"No. It's a pretty shitty one if it is."

Deathly silence answered me. "I told you about how new vampires aren't supposed to turn others, right?"

I rubbed the back of my neck. "Yes."

"You did it anyway."

"Yes."

There was another pause. "I hope you have a really good excuse, D," she finally said. "I'm on my way." She hung up without giving me a chance to say anything else.

Sighing, I put my phone back in my pocket and walked into the living room. I found Cassandra on her feet. She smiled sheepishly. "May I take a shower? I'd really like to get cleaned up."

I mentally kicked myself for not offering sooner. "Of course," I said and showed her to the bathroom, pointing out where everything was and explaining the quirks of my shower controls.

Back in the living room, I paced while trying to figure

out what the hell I was going to tell Sadie. I had to tell her the truth, and it was going to have to be enough. What would she do? Was there some kind of punishment for this? To keep myself from pacing, I plopped onto the edge of my sofa, drumming my heels and waiting for the hangman.

The thump on the door announced my untimely end. I barely got to it before she let herself in and without preamble smacked me on the side of my head as she passed. "Okay, what the hell happened and where are they?"

I gestured to the couch sarcastically. "Be my guest. She's in the shower." Flopping onto the couch and realizing this wasn't going to be a haul-me-to-jail kind of thing, I sat back and gave the whole jumbled, insufferable ordeal.

She was quiet for a while, wheels visibly turning in her head, before she let out a resigned sigh. "What's done is done. I suppose you didn't really have a choice. No one wants to watch someone else die."

The bathroom door opened, and Cassandra stepped out, wearing just a towel. Her eyes widened when she saw Sadie. "I didn't realize... There are no clothes... I didn't want to put back on the bloody ones."

"Oh, right, I have some of my ex's stuff in my room." I started to get up, but Sadie pushed me back down.

"You're in the doghouse. No treats for you," she said in a low tone and then turned a pleasant smile to Cassandra. "I'm Sadie Stanton. I work with D."

Cassandra tilted her head. "You're a vampire."

My boss smiled, impressed. "It usually takes new vampires longer to develop that sense." There were only two doors and my new vampire had come out of one, so it was obvious where the bedroom was. "I'm sure I can help you find some clothes."

Cassandra nodded uncertainly, casting a glance at me before following. I felt kind of like a kid being forced to sit out recess. For a moment, I considered arguing with my boss rummaging in my room, but I was already in enough trouble.

After a while, they came back out. Cassandra was wearing Raven's clothes, but she was taller and leaner so the dark jeans were too short and the black Ozz Fest T-shirt a little baggy. Still, she looked good. I began to get the idea she could wear a garbage bag and make it look like fashion week.

Sadie had Cassandra laughing, albeit timidly, about something as they walked into the room. I had gotten to my feet when the ladies re-entered—blame my Southern roots. I felt dumb. "Feeling better?"

"Much," Cassandra said with a shy smile, "thank you. Although these aren't quite the type of clothes I'd usually wear."

"Yeah, my ex is kind of a walking disaster."

Sadie looked me up and down. "Like you're one to talk, always dressed in black. Hell, even your undershirt is black. I bet your underwear is, too."

I frowned, strangely embarrassed. "I don't really think it's appropriate to talk about a man's underwear when you're his boss."

She shrugged. "After several decades, you stop caring about these things." She smirked. "I'm going back to the office." Turning to Cassandra, she said, "You seem to be handling things all right, but feel free to call me if you need anything. It was a pleasure meeting you, and welcome to the club." To me, "Walk me out."

I nodded and followed obediently. Just outside the door, she turned to me. "Are you going to be okay?"

"Guess I have no choice, huh?" I figured honesty was best here. "It's going to be...weird, for lack of a better term. She seems much more level-headed than I was, so I think we'll manage."

"Yeah, she does seem to be handling it all right." She

nodded thoughtfully, but her dark brows drew down in a little frown.

"What?" I asked warily.

She shook her head. "Nothing," she said, but the frown persisted. "She's just handling it a little *too* well. It's odd is all. Even the most prepared fledglings have some kind of reaction to their own death and rebirth, but she's not showing the usual signs. It could just be shock, though. It will probably hit her later. Call me if you need me." She paused again. "Do you want to sit out your schedule for a couple days?"

Instinct wanted to say yes, but then I thought of Sarah and her grieving clients having to face the bigots alone. I shook my head. "No, I'll keep my jobs."

Sadie smiled approvingly. "Hang in there. You know where to find me."

Chapter Seventeen

I returned to Cassandra and sat with her, but I had no idea what to say. It was like the first date from hell, where you went out for drinks and then moved in together.

I had a vampire in my house.

What was I supposed to do with her now?

The expression on her face said she felt the same way, so at least I wasn't alone. It helped, a little.

"We should probably, you know, get to know one another," she suggested, slowly rubbing her hands together. "I suppose that part usually comes before the blood and all that, but better late than never?" She smiled. The expression lit her eyes up.

"Yeah, I suppose so." I chuckled nervously. I was glad vampires were spared the anxious indignity of perspiration. Score one for the dead guy. "I don't really know that there's much to tell. I was born in Alabama and moved up here for work. I only got turned a couple of weeks ago, so I'm not even really qualified to *be* a vampire, let alone make one."

Her smile didn't waver. "What do you do for work?"

I shrugged. "Originally, I was in IT. I quit that job after I got turned." I paused. "I was kind of in an epic sulk at that point. I went to Sadie, and she hired me at her agency. I do some stuff with their computers because they aren't good with them, and then I've been going to appointments with their animator. There are some protesters giving her and her clients trouble. I stand around looking mean and keep them from fucking with her while she works."

"That sounds like a good thing to do." She nodded. "Are they, like, LOHAV and PAAS and such?"

"I guess. I don't ask for their credentials. Seems like the type though, right?"

LOHAV I've already told you about, but as it happens, they aren't the only anti-preternatural group out there. They're just the biggest and the angriest. The next on the list is the People's Army Against the Supernatural. Funny, they have the word 'army' in their name, but according to Sadie, they just wage wars on paper. If I had to pick between the two for who was showing up to be obnoxious to Sarah, then I would definitely guess LOHAV.

"Feels kind of weird, though," I surprised myself by confessing. "I wasn't really a fan of the preternatural before becoming one myself. I mean, I never went so far as to join one of those groups, and I didn't necessarily agree with the violence, but I wasn't comfortable with vampires and werewolves running around alongside me at the grocery store." I didn't know why I told her that. It wasn't something I was proud of, and given the circumstances, I would rather she have a good image of me.

She didn't look upset, or like she was judging me. She rested her arm along the back of the couch and leaned her head against her hand. "Then how did you end up becoming one of them?"

Her expression was so incredibly...open and earnest. I wasn't entirely sure how to handle it, but my brain apparently decided for me. I just started talking again. "It wasn't exactly by choice." I looked away, stopping myself with a sigh. How not to sound like a skirt-chasing douchebag... "I guess I was just stupid, hooking up with a woman I didn't know. I knew she was a vampire, she was hot, and I'd just broken up with my girlfriend. I could have done without the fang bit, but the rest was hard to ignore. But then, after we'd... Well, you get the idea..." For some reason, I felt weird saying 'it' to her. Like a middle school kid again or something. "She bit me, then kissed me after biting her lip. Before I figured out what had happened, she broke my neck. Woke up the next night like this."

Cassandra frowned sympathetically and reached over to lightly touch my hand, and the small gesture of comfort did make me feel better about the whole wretched experience. "That's terrible," she said softly. "You must have been upset."

I snorted. "I don't think 'upset' really begins to cover it. It was like someone had lit me on fire and turned me into a tornado with shiny new fangs. She tried to explain why she'd done it, but I never gave her the chance." I paused and finally met her eye again. "And now I never will."

"Is she dead?" Her question startled me, and I was sure it showed because she blushed faintly. "It's just the way you said it, made it sound...really permanent."

"Yeah, she is," I said with a slow nod. "I talked about it a little with a mutual sort of friend. She had some trouble following her and for some reason thought I could help, but her trouble got to her before I bothered to find out."

She was quiet for a few moments. "You seem like the type to protect people," she said. She had the most unnerving ability to surprise me in such a short span of time.

Frowning, I looked at her for a while. "You think?"

"Well, the woman who turned you obviously had some reason for it, and then Sadie hired you to help the animator, and you saved me," she pointed out what probably should have been obvious. I'd not given it that much thought.

"I suppose." I wasn't ready to admit it was anything but coincidence. We'd been talking about me the whole time, and my catching on to this helped spur the conversation along. "What about you? I should probably know something about the woman living in my apartment."

If saying it so bluntly freaked her out, she didn't let it show. She pulled her hand back and shrugged, sinking a little into the couch. "There's not that much to tell about me either. I was born and raised here. I was a student at Three Rivers Community College, studying to be a nurse."

I caught the past tense. "They have all kinds of allowances for the supernatural these days, including night classes. You don't have to quit just because you've become a vampire."

She shook her head. "I dropped out last semester. I had some…troubles at home that were just too much to add school to and my grades were dropping."

"Oh." My size-thirteen boot tasted like ass right then. "You could go back, since you're not, you know, home anymore. And I read somewhere that they are trying to pick up more preternatural students, so the vampire thing could work in your favor."

Smiling faintly, she nodded. "I suppose I could," she agreed, "but maybe I should get used to being a preternatural first." She paused and frowned. "Once I've got a handle on all the changes, I'll get a job. You are really nice to let me stay here, but I won't just take up space and not give anything back. I promise."

Truth be told, I hadn't even thought of it. I was getting used to the idea of her being here and kind of liking it. Still, I didn't want to get in the way of an independent woman thing. "Oh, sure, but get your bearings first. But hey, the vampire thing cuts down on the usual bills."

"I can imagine it does." She laughed softly. "Not as much on food, right?"

"Right." I paused, on the verge of running out of things to say, but then I thought to add, "You can take the bedroom, by the way. It's not really as dirty as it looks. I just never pick up the laundry." Okay, that sounded bad. "Other than that, though, it's fairly decent."

She bit her lip. "I don't want to kick you out of your room." She hesitated. "Is the living room even secure, from the sun and all?" Turning, she looked at my curtains.

I appreciated her concern. "Don't worry," I said. "The curtains block out the sun, and the couch is perfectly comfortable. I've slept off hangovers often enough on it. It's okay. Take the bed."

If she was going to protest further, she didn't have the chance.

There was a knock at the door.

CHAPTER EIGHTEEN

Curiously, I got to my feet and answered it. The person on the other side was certainly no one I had been expecting.

"Raven." This was an unpleasant surprise. "What the hell are you doing here?"

"You haven't called me since you blew everyone off," she said. The words seemed like something she'd say when she was pissed, but she didn't *look* pissed. In fact, she looked... I didn't think I'd ever seen that look on her face. She stepped over the threshold and had her hands fisting my shirt before I could stop her. "You become a vampire, which is the hottest thing you've ever done in your life, and you don't call me?"

I was too shocked to pry her off, or try to recall from that week of new vampire funk if I had *told* anyone what had happened... "The fuck?" Really, it was the first thing that came into my head as she leaned in way too close, her shitty perfume doing a number on my enhanced senses, and my super sight seeing all the terrible details of her excessive make-up. For a moment, I briefly wished I was human again so I didn't have to see this crap.

She pouted, and I couldn't take my eyes off the smudges in her black lipstick or where it faded away at the inside of her lips. "Don't be like that, D. I know things kind of ended bad, but come on. The vampire thing is great. I want you to tell me *all* about it."

When she started pushing me back into the apartment, fingers still clenched around my shirt, I found my spine again and stopped. "Wait just a damn minute." I broke her look and found words other than 'fuck' and 'damn.' "I thought I was very clear about needing to cut ties with everyone. You and I had already ended that dance before this even happened. My getting vamped did not change my relief at breaking it off."

"Why does it have to mean you don't see any of us anymore?" She skirted around the 'me' part—like always. Her pout deepened, and she tugged at her shirt to show off more skin. Fucking pathetic, really.

My palms rubbed at my temples in the universal sign of 'I-can't-fucking-believe-this.' "It's a new life—" Well, not really. "—and I have to start over again. If I keep hanging around you pulsing fleshbags, I'll either keep trying to fake human or wind up seeing you fucks as entrees on the menu." Reaching down, I tried to gently pry her fingers away from my clothing. I was still only wearing the A-shirt, and it let her get closer to my skin than I wanted.

"Come on," she said, leaning into me. "I promise you'll be very happy to be a vampire when you're with me." She smiled.

It took me a moment, but then it dawned on me what was going on here. She was trying to seduce me. I hadn't recognized it because she'd never done it before. I'd been a much easier mark in the past. Flash your tits and I was good.

I kinda figured she'd been pretty hot for the newly legal supernatural men out there, as many of our crowd were, but this tipped the scale.

"No," I said, putting my hands on her shoulders and pushing her back a step. My arms were longer than hers, and she had to let go now. I was a lot stronger than her, though I was trying to take it as easily as I could. "Not only no, but hell no. You wanted to be a conniving bitch, and I was determined to be miserable. Not anymore. Yeah, okay, the bloodsucking thing gets you slicker than owl shit, but it doesn't do a whole lot for me, so why don't you leave and go find one of those vamp Lotharios they write about these days."

"D," she whined and wouldn't let me push her out without more force than I was comfortable with. I wanted her gone, not through the wall. Besides, the landlord would make me pay for that. "Just let me come in."

Somehow, she managed to get by my super vampire prowess, but only as far as the living room. She stopped dead on her platforms when she saw Cassandra, sitting placidly on the couch. Cassandra lifted her head and looked at Raven, then at me, then back at Raven. A strange look passed through her eyes, like a predator evaluating new prey. Apparently, she found Raven wanting because the look changed to confusion.

"Hello?" she asked uncertainly.

"Who the hell is that?!" Raven demanded, turning on me.

"Not a damn bit of your business." I grabbed her shoulder and started steering her out. She resisted, so I picked her up off the ground and deposited her in the hallway, shutting the door behind me.

I walked back into the living room and dropped to the couch beside Cassandra with a sigh. She bit her lip and didn't say anything for a while.

Finally, she did ask, "Who was that?"

"Psychotic ex-girlfriend," I replied, staring straight ahead.

"The one whose clothes I'm wearing?"

"That would be the one."

"I see."

Neither of us said anything for a while then. I just thought about how damned odd it was. Why had she shown up on my doorstep now? It had been more than a week since I had dropped the message to people. Then again, I'd never really understood Raven, so why should I have expected to now? Did I expect some great wisdom to descend upon me just because I was dead? I'd skipped the whole White Light experience, after all, so I obviously skipped the Greater Understanding as well.

"Are you all right?" Cassandra broke through my thoughts.

"Hmm? Oh, yes. I'm fine. I'm just trying to understand…" I wasn't exactly sure what I was trying to understand.

"Women?" she suggested with a small smile. "It's never going to happen. I'd give up now."

That got me to laugh. "You have me there." I scrubbed a hand through my hair. I will say this for the vampire thing, the hair doesn't get as dirty as fast. Less bodily oils to worry about. "I'm sorry about that. Hopefully, she won't try that again."

Cassandra shrugged. "It didn't bother me. It was just kind of strange." She paused and ran her fingers through the ends of her hair. "Do you mind if I ask what happened between the two of you?"

I didn't mind, but I wasn't sure how to explain. I wasn't entirely sure what had happened, other than it had ended. "I think we weren't ever really happy with each other, but just ended up with each other 'cause we hung out with the same people. You know how it goes."

"Not really," she admitted with an attractively shy smile. "I haven't dated much."

That surprised me. She was very lovely and very nice. I'd have thought she would have men trailing after her everywhere she went. "Nothing to be embarrassed about," I said, instead of the things I was thinking. "Dating is hell. Being dead doesn't save you."

She laughed softly. "I can see that," she agreed. "Crazy ex-girlfriends aside, I hope I'm not keeping you from anything?"

I pulled my phone from my pocket and checked the time. "I will have to head out shortly for a job, but they usually don't last long." I put it back. "Will you be okay here on your own for a bit?"

"Oh, I'll be fine." She nodded. "I promise I won't mess up any of your stuff." Humor glimmered briefly in her eyes.

I grinned, perhaps for the first time in a while. "It's not like any of my stuff is worth messing with. I'm not worried."

Chapter Nineteen

Fortunately, the job that night went easily. It was actually two appointments back-to-back. There was no unwanted company for the first, and those that were at the second took one look at me and stayed in their car. I was okay with that.

After those were done, I stopped at the butcher's on the way home. If there were going to be two new vampires in my apartment, we'd need it.

Despite the ease and quickness of the night's work, I'd been on edge. I tried to keep it to myself, but I was sure Sarah picked up on some of it. Everything had just happened so fast the past two nights. Hell, the past two weeks. It was taking some time to process. I only had so much RAM to burn, you know? And it's not like you can upgrade your brain, human or vampire.

My 'oh shit' meter pinged when I approached the apartment and saw the door sitting open. I hurried inside, only to slip on something on the floor and land hard on my back. Vampire reflexes, my ass.

"Oh no! Are you okay?" It was Cassandra's voice.

I sat up, cursing when I put my hand down on glass shards and blood on the patch of tile in front of my door. Frowning, I looked at her. She also sat on the floor, pale eyes wide, with blood on her chin and shirt and hands.

"Are *you* okay?" I asked, alarm singing loudly in me. "What happened?"

She bit her lip and looked sheepish, like a confused kid. "I don't know."

I blinked. "You don't know?"

"No, I don't know." She shook her head. "I thought I heard someone at the door as I came from the kitchen with a jar. I must have opened it to see and then slipped. My head really hurts. I think I hit it." She looked like she was about to cry, and maybe she would have if vampires could. "Must have broken the jar. I'm really sorry."

"It's all right," I assured her quickly. "I guess maybe you don't remember 'cause you hit your head. I've heard that can happen. Do you want to see a doctor or something?" I knew they had doctors specializing in our kind, though I couldn't imagine what that crash course over the past year must have looked like.

She shook her head. "I'm okay, really." Cassandra pressed a hand to her forehead, leaving a bloody palm print on her skin. Her shoulders rose and fell with a deep sigh before she looked at me again. The frightened expression was gone. "I'm...sorry," she said uncertainly, but then shook her head. "I wish I knew what happened." She surveyed the floor and then saw my hand. Grabbing it before I could stop her, she quickly and delicately plucked the shards out of my skin.

Once the obstructions were clear, my vampire healing quickly took care of the rest. "Thanks," I said quietly.

On some kind of instinct of my own, I reached out and gently touched her temple, concerned. "Are you going to be okay?"

She touched the back of my hand with the same light touch. "I'll be fine. It's not the first time I've taken a blow to the head, though I didn't have vampire stamina then." She smiled, but it was a dark expression.

I sensed there was more to that statement than she was

saying, but I didn't ask. I didn't think we knew one another well enough to go that deep yet. That kind of dark only came from something major.

After a moment, we both dropped our hands. I got to my feet and offered her a hand up. "We should get this cleaned." I headed into the kitchen for some paper towels and the trashcan.

Between the two of us, we got it taken care of and then got ourselves clean as well. We didn't talk much while we worked, but I kept sneaking glances at her, because I was worried. She was really nice, and I didn't want to see anything else happen to her. And she was my first fledgling, so I didn't need my vampire permanent record somewhere marked up.

Look at him. He couldn't even keep his first fledgling undamaged for one day.

Clean and back on the couch, I apparently kept staring because finally she half-laughed and asked, "What?"

I frowned. "Are you *sure* you're okay?"

"Yes, I'm fine." She sighed, but smiled a little. "I promise."

Unless I wanted her to smack me, I knew I had to stop asking. I wasn't as convinced as she was, but what did I know? It was her body and her head. If she said she was fine, then she probably was. Vampires are a bit tougher than humans, after all.

"Well," I said, uncertainly, "I'm done with work for the night, and we've a few hours till dawn. What would you like to do?"

"Honestly?" Her smile was a little wistful. I nodded. "I think I'd just like to lie down and watch television. I didn't know vampires could get tired, but I am. It's been a lot to handle tonight."

I felt like an idiot for not being more aware of that. "Of course." I nodded and found the remote under the couch. "Watch whatever you like. I'm just going to be on the computer." It was all in the same room, so it wasn't like I'd be going that far.

We then settled into what had to be the most normal domestic routine two people like us could fall into. Hell, it would be normal for other people too. She watched some late-night *Lifetime* movie I worked hard to ignore and yet couldn't stop looking at from time to time, while I played *World of Warcraft.*

I logged into my night elf rogue and played out some mindless heroics, died a few times, and cussed out (in my head) the inept priest. The way that many people played night elves like vampires in this game (generally in Goldshire) had taken on a whole new depth lately, but I tried to ignore it.

"What server?"

Cassandra scared the shit out of me, just appearing behind me like that when I hadn't even heard her get off the couch, and I ran my character into a pack of mobs, was toasted before I could use any of my escape tricks, and got yelled at by the party leader.

"Sorry," she said, but an amused smile tugged her lips.

"Right." I gave her a dirty look, but knew there wasn't much heat to it. "So, you play?"

She nodded. "Can you guess?"

I narrowed my eyes. "Priest."

"Very good. Race?"

"Just tell me not Horde."

She laughed. "Alliance," she reassured me. "Human priestess. And I have a low-level gnome warlock that I don't play very often. The pets following thing bugs me for some reason, but if I unsummon them, then I don't have them when something squishes my clothie ass."

I laughed. "We'll have to play some time. Maybe I'll create a dwarf paladin to follow you instead and cover that clothie ass. Maybe I'll be less annoying than an imp."

"Maybe," she agreed. Her smile lost some flavor for a moment, but then returned and she rested a hand on my shoulder. "I'm going to go to bed. I know dawn is still a little ways off, but I just want to lie down and relax before it comes."

"Sure thing." I nodded, although I was sad to see her go away, even if it was only to the bedroom. "I'll see you tomorrow."

After she left, I finished what I was doing and logged out, heading for the couch.

Dawn was near.

Chapter Twenty

I knew something was different the moment sunset woke me. Groggily, I tried to figure out what it was and became aware of a weight pressing against the left side of my body. I pried my eyes open and looked down. To my great surprise, I found Cassandra lying there. Surprise gave way to confusion.

How had she gotten out here? For some reason, I wasn't as concerned with why, as it was nice to wake up beside someone, but how did she do it? I didn't understand the exact mechanics, but I knew that the younger the vampire, the longer into the sunset they slept and the earlier at sunrise they went down. It had to do with magic rather than biology, I was sure.

She appeared to be in the daylight coma, and I would have hated to wake her, but I knew only the sun had control over this.

In a few minutes, she came to.

"How did I get here?" She didn't seem concerned, just confused like I was.

"You mean you don't know?" I frowned. "I imagine you'd know better than me."

"I sort of remember it," she said, "but it's foggy, like a dream."

I thought about this. I also noticed neither of us was moving, but I wasn't going to point that out. "Maybe there's some kind of vampire sleepwalking during those gray moments at dawn and dusk."

"I suppose that could make sense," she granted. "Perhaps you should ask your boss about it." I nodded, and she continued, "I hope you don't mind." She gazed up, leaving me with vague images of animals from Disney movies. It wasn't like she was trying to give me the big-eyed look, I could usually recognize that. It was more of a passive thing with her. It was just the way she looked.

"No, no, I don't mind," I reassured her quickly. "I was a little surprised."

"I feel safe around you." I liked that she explained without making me ask. "I guess I feel it from my subconscious too, since I did it unconsciously." She laid her head back against my shoulder for a moment. It looked like she was listening to my heartbeat, but I knew that wasn't the case.

After a few moments, she got up. I realized she was wearing one of my T-shirts. I didn't mind at all. I didn't mind that she wasn't wearing any pants either. My shirt was so long on her it was practically a short dress, but it worked. I tried not to stare as she walked into the bedroom, presumably to put on more clothes.

After a few minutes, she emerged from the bedroom with an armful and headed straight into the bathroom. I heard the shower running. I elected to skip the shower again. I'd live scrubby. She came out a little while later, wearing yesterday's jeans, but one of my T-shirts.

"Are you hungry?" I tried not to think about how good that looked on her.

"I had enough yesterday." She smiled and shook her head, wet blonde hair waving around her face with the motion. "I actually, I wanted to ask..." She hesitated.

I waited for her to start again, but she kind of seemed to zone out. Or at least, retreat deep in her mind. "You wanted to ask?" I gently prompted after a few moments.

She blinked. "Sorry. Yes. I wanted to ask if you would mind going home with me." She frowned prettily. "I don't want to go home to stay, but I would like to get some of my things. I don't want to go by myself, though. Would you go with me?"

After the way she had reacted to the suggestion yesterday, the request surprised me, but I guessed she couldn't live in old clothes of Raven's and my T-shirts forever. "Sure, that's no problem. I'm clear for a couple hours."

☾○☽

We drove to her house in silence. It was on the other side of town, so I figured driving would be better than walking.

At one point, I did try to ask some of the questions on my mind. "So, can I ask why it is you don't want to go home?"

She didn't reply for a long time, looking out the window. For a moment, I thought she hadn't heard me. "You can ask, but I'd rather not talk about it."

It wasn't much of an answer, but I didn't feel right pressing.

As we got closer, she gave me directions for the side streets until we got to a two-story house with the door at the top of a set of stairs, directly into the second floor with the garage door below. I parked in the short driveway and got out of the car. I then realized Cassandra hadn't moved yet.

I gave her a few moments before opening her door for her.

"Are you coming?" I asked gently. My suspicions yesterday about the deep darkness felt confirmed. I had seen enough movies and watched enough news to make a few guesses, but I didn't want to presume either. So, I just added, "We'll make it quick, I promise." I felt a strong urge to take care of her, to bundle her up and make it better.

Smiling tremulously up at me, she nodded and climbed out. We went up the stairs, and she walked in. The door was unlocked. I followed her into a kitchen.

Immediately, my vampire sense of smell was overwhelmed by the stench. The sink was filled with dirty dishes in a mound, and there was a loaf of moldy bread on the counter next to a bowl of what I thought were apples. I had never been an obsessively clean person, but even I didn't let it get this bad.

Cassandra paid it no attention, just walked forward. I followed through a similarly messy living room and cluttered hallway to a room at the end. She pulled a key out of her pocket and unlocked a door, letting me in and locking it again behind us.

This room, a bedroom, was incredibly clean. It was all in white and blue. It looked like a girl's room.

Opening the closet, she pulled a backpack from the top shelf. Even her closet was clean, with no clutter on the floor. She tossed the bag on the bed and a small suitcase followed. I stood uselessly while she methodically went through the room, picking and choosing clothing by a method I couldn't fathom and putting neatly folded items into the suitcase. A small white wicker basket of girly stuff went into a smaller zippered bag and into the suitcase. I had to admit I was enthralled by the process, unable to look away.

A laptop went into the backpack followed by a short stack of spiral notebooks. A few delicate items were wrapped in clothing and put into the suitcase. Then she stopped in front of a bookshelf. There was just one, but it was six foot high and filled. Now, she frowned and stared.

"I don't know which ones to take. I want them all."

I looked them over. There were several novels, mostly romance and fantasy, and then some large medical texts. "If you have a box, we'll take them all. We're vampires, remember? We're strong. I could carry a box of these without too much trouble."

Her face lit up, and I felt like I'd just won the lottery.

She hurried out of the room with half-vampire speed and came back with a folded box that had once belonged to a computer, a desktop by the size of it. She used duct tape to turn it back into a box, and we filled it with the books and then added some more of her clothing. She seemed to own very little, so we were able to get everything but the furniture and bedding in the big box, two suitcases, and a backpack.

Inhaling deeply, she looked pleased. I took one trip to the car with the big box and the bigger suitcase on top. Weight-wise, I could have taken them all, but being a vampire didn't change certain laws of physics. I still had to navigate awkward like everyone else.

I came back in the house and took the last suitcase. She had the backpack on. We were making our getaway when the kitchen door opened and a man walked in. He had Cassandra's coloring but was my size and as messy as the house.

"Cassie!" he said, clearly shocked. His expression darkened. "Where the hell have you been, girl?"

CHAPTER TWENTY-ONE

I instantly bristled at the tone and the way he looked at her.

She inhaled and tilted her chin up. "None of your business. All you need to know is that I'm leaving."

He stepped toward her. "Like hell you are." He turned on me. "Who is this?"

She held her ground. "You don't own me. I can go where I like and with whom I like, and who he is isn't your concern."

To this, he didn't seem to have anything to say, but he stared at her silently for a long, dark moment. I could feel her shrinking in on herself. She took a step back and got that look on her face like when I came home and slipped in the blood. "Daddy, no," she said weakly.

He smiled. "Now be a good girl and put your stuff back."

At that point, I don't know if she would have resisted or done it. It didn't matter.

You know that voice in your head, the one that tells you when to do or not to do something because it might not be a good idea? I don't always have one, or it isn't very loud. I had her small suitcase in both hands and used it to shove Cassandra's father back against the counter. I wanted to punch that smile into the back of his skull. I could do it, too.

Under my weight, his back bent against the edge of the counter until his head smacked into the cabinet.

"You don't need to know who I am. Wouldn't matter a damn bit if you did. Cassandra wants out of here, so we're leaving. If I see your fucking face ever again..." I pressed the edge of the luggage against the underside of his chin, forcing his head as far back as it would go until he started coughing.

Cassandra bolted past me. I glared at him for a moment longer. I could feel my incisors digging into my bottom teeth, so I bared them. His eyes were wider than I'd ever seen on a man, and it made me feel (sickeningly) good. I clicked my teeth, chomping at the air a hairsbreadth from his nose, then left. I didn't even bother looking over my shoulder to make sure we weren't followed. Thundering my way out to the car and slinging her suitcase into the trunk, I was doing all I could to control my urge to go back there and make a meal out of him.

When I got into the car, I found her hugging herself with her head against the window. I felt maybe now I needed to press a little. First things first, we had to get out of there. So, I started the car and drove off.

☾○☽

I drove for a little while, taking my time, and gave her a chance to unfold. If we'd still been human, this would have been a good time to stop for a cup of coffee. I wasn't sure a jar of blood would have the same effect. Instead, I found a quiet corner street and parked.

Turning her head, she looked at me questioningly.

"So, you want to tell me what's going on?" I asked.

"Not particularly." She smiled weakly.

I shook my head with a sympathetic expression. "I'm not gonna pry if you're gonna stonewall. Your life, your business, all that jazz. But you are staying in my apartment, and I did just jack a guy into a cabinet and threaten bodily harm. I probably shouldn't have done it, but oh fucking well, there it is. So I'm going to ask, is there anything I need to know?"

Turning back to the window, she didn't reply for a while. "There's just some bad shit between me and my father. There's *a lot* of shit between me and my father." She sighed and pressed her fingertips to the glass. "You do deserve to know, but I would really rather not get into the details. It's just bad, and I needed to get out of there."

"Is that why you were out the other night, when I found you?" It seemed kind of obvious now. She had been running away. I could understand that.

"Yeah, it is." She nodded and dropped her hands into her lap. "I left the house in a hurry, which is why I didn't have any of my stuff and wasn't really paying attention to where I ended up."

I let that all sink in and nodded slowly. "Think he'll try to come after you?" I didn't really need her to tell me the gory details, but I did need to know if there was going to be a safety issue. I needed to keep the both of us safe, and we did have a major weakness with daylight.

She shook her head without hesitating. "He's not like that. He's a coward. I'm sure you scared the shit out of him." Cassandra laughed, but there was no mirth to it.

"What about your mom?" I asked what I thought was the next logical question.

"She died when I was six." She looked at her hands, palms up like she was waiting for something to fall into them. "I have an older sister, but she moved out years ago. I haven't heard from her since. I think she's in California somewhere now, but I can't be sure."

I thought about this for a moment, looking out the windshield and drumming my thumbs on the steering wheel. I felt really bad for her. "You got a kind of shitty family." I sighed.

She laughed again. There was something kind of chilling

in a laugh with so little humor to it. "I guess you could say that."

We were silent for a while. I knew I'd started the conversation, but now I wasn't entirely sure what to say. I wasn't a counselor. The deep dark apparently went really deep. I found myself hoping she might trust me enough to confide in me some time, but I understood that today wasn't that day.

After a moment, I asked, "Do you need anything?" Pause. "Can I do anything?"

Her smile had more warmth to it this time. She reached across the center console and put her arm on mine. "I'm all right now, but thank you." She took her hand back and brushed her hair over her shoulder. "I'm just sorry you ended up in the middle of this mess I've been calling a life."

I waved a hand. "Don't worry about it. I'd like to think I helped a little, and that's a good thing. Besides, my life isn't perfect. Maybe we can figure things out from here better together than alone." I didn't know where that shit had come from, but I meant it.

She seemed to like the sentiment, because her smile deepened and she nodded. "I think so."

I didn't know what it was about her, but there was just something. Eloquent descriptions aren't my strong suit, so it was hard then to describe what it was, but she had a unique effect on me, and I liked whatever it was I felt. I wondered if maybe it was the vampire thing, if there was a bond between sire and fledgling.

Would I have ever felt it with Cielle, if she hadn't been murdered? It was a good question. Maybe Cassandra was just special. She seemed special.

"So..." She pulled me out of my thoughts. "Where to now? Should we go home and unpack my shit? I'll stuff it in a corner so it won't take up your space."

I chuckled, strangely pleased by hearing her say 'home' that way. "Don't worry about that. It's not like I don't have enough room or that much stuff of my own." I paused and smiled a little. "Besides, we have to get your laptop set up so you can run some instances with me."

Still, I felt a little unsettled after the encounter with her father, even if it didn't show. I didn't really feel like heading right home.

"Let's stop for a drink first, though," I said, starting the car back up.

Chapter Twenty-Two

She didn't object, so I drove to 5. I wasn't entirely sure why I wanted to go there, but then again, I didn't know any other good fang dives. She looked out the window curiously as we pulled into the parking lot and found a spot.

"Where are we?" she asked.

"Five," I answered as we got out of the car and I locked it behind us. After all, her shit was in there. "It's a vampire bar." I'm sure I didn't look happy the way I said it, judging by the dubious look she gave me. "It's kinda like a second birthplace," I muttered.

Cassandra nodded, and we walked up to the door. I opened it for her, and she smiled appreciatively. We walked in and emerged from the hall to the goings-on of a vampire bar, and I began to doubt my choice to come here, but she didn't seem too disturbed. We headed straight for the bar.

Quintus came right up to us. He nodded at me and then looked at Cassandra. His mouth opened, like he was about to say something, but he paused and smiled in a way I didn't think I'd ever seen. He offered his hand across the bar. "Quintus."

"Cassandra," she replied, smiling back. It was obvious they liked each other right off. "So, you named the bar after yourself?"

He rumbled a deep chuckle. "I did. I have a fondness for the number."

Her eyes stared at him for an unnervingly long time, tilting her head. "I hope it's not offensive to point out a vampire's age." Her tone was thoughtful.

"Not usually. Why, what can you tell?" He tossed his dishrag over his shoulder.

"You're powerful. You're hundreds of years old." She narrowed her eyes slightly, like she was deep in thought. "Quintus is an ancient Roman name, means five. Were you the fifth child?"

He folded his tree trunk arms over his chest. "Few have put the name and the origin together so quickly *and* unaided. I'm impressed. Yes, I was the fifth child. And I am old."

She giggled, pleased she'd gotten it right. "Fair enough."

I watched in amazement. I wasn't really sure why I was amazed, Cassandra was a sweet girl, and it wasn't like Quintus was some kind of monster she'd just soothed, but still, the exchange amazed me.

"Where did you find her?" Quintus turned his attention to me.

I blinked and looked at her. I didn't really know how much of it she would want me to say, but she solved that dilemma.

"He saved me when I was being attacked," she said with a smile in my direction. "He turned me so I wouldn't die permanently."

"I see." Quintus nodded, giving me a rather significant look.

I wondered what he was thinking. Was he thinking about how I managed to save Cassandra but had abandoned Cielle? I tried to resist the sudden wash of guilt, to little effect. But whatever he thought, he kept it very well to himself as he poured two glasses of blood and passed them to each of us.

They shared a few more companionable words while I sipped my drink, but then realized we'd drawn the attention of...well, the entire bar. Almost everyone had stopped what they were doing and were watching us. I felt an odd twitch between my shoulder blades, because I knew they weren't looking at me. They were looking at *her*. I had to resist a very strong urge to body-block their undead gazes.

Thus far, I seemed to be the only one who noticed, and no one had moved or done anything. They just stared. I stared back, but it didn't seem to bother anyone like it bothered me. I guess I wasn't that intimidating with this crowd. Still, I intended to keep an eye on them.

"So, D..." Quintus grabbed my attention again. "I understand you are now under the employ of Ms. Stanton."

"You hear a lot." I half-smiled. I imagined he knew a lot more than he let on.

"It serves me well." He smiled back. In fact, he'd smiled more in the five minutes we'd been there than I'd seen in all the times before. "Would it make you more comfortable to know I do not know the details of your employment?"

I laughed a little and drank my blood. "Right now, she has me going out with the animator on appointments. There's been some trouble lately, so I'm there to guard her and keep the crazies from getting at Sarah or her clients."

"A worthy job," he approved, nodding.

I glanced back over my shoulder and now saw that a few vampires had started to get a little closer. What was their deal? I looked at Cassandra, but she didn't seem to notice. I wasn't sure if I should be worried or not.

When I turned back, Cassandra's hand was across the bar and resting on Quintus's arm with a smile. "I hope some day you'll tell me. You must have a fascinating history."

"I shall consider it in earnest." He smiled back *again*. I wondered if I should be jealous.

I also wondered if I should be paranoid. Every time I glanced back over my shoulder, they seemed a little closer.

Now Quintus glanced up, and his smile instantly turned into a frown. He seemed to just be tuning into the show behind me. "Would you two care for a little more privacy to continue our conversation?" His eyes remained on the crowd.

Cassandra blinked and glanced over her shoulder, then shrunk back a little.

I had an instant and irrational knee-jerk I-don't-want-to reaction to the backroom but realized it would perhaps be for the best. We could leave, but we might be followed. "Yeah, that might be a good idea." I thought about slipping out the window once we were in there.

With Quintus looking curiously, and warily, at the others, I ushered Cassandra into the back and shut the door behind us.

"What was that about?" she asked, bewildered.

"I don't know." I stared at the door, but nothing happened so I turned back to her. "I guess they thought you were pretty, or maybe they just like new people." It had to be more than that, but I didn't want to worry her. Maybe it was just some creepy vampire thing I wasn't familiar with yet.

She looked about as convinced as I was, but we sat on the couch. I felt that initial reaction to the room come back. I glanced around with a frown.

"What is it?"

"This is the room where I was turned," I explained, surprised at myself for saying it so easily. "It's not a good memory."

She laid her hand on my arm, and I instantly felt better. "It's all right now," she said softly. She smiled placidly at me. I didn't see any trace of the confused, saddened girl that had been there after we'd left her father's house. That smile could have soothed the most savage of beasts. "You're here with me."

I tried to talk, but my vocal cords wouldn't work, so I

nodded instead. The room had no more power over me.

It amazed me what a pretty girl could do.

Before anything more was said, there was a brief commotion outside the door.

CHAPTER TWENTY-THREE

I got to my feet, ready to go see what it was, but the door opened before I had the chance. Quintus burst in and slammed the door behind him.

"My apologies," he rumbled quietly. His face was gathering storm clouds. "I had to eject an obnoxious customer, and he did not take too kindly to it."

"What the hell is going on here tonight, Quintus?" I asked.

He waved a hand. "Damned if I know. Our kind can have their...peculiarities. I think perhaps there is something in the air."

It was at this point that I noticed the blood running down his arm from what looked like a ragged bitemark. I pointed at it. "What the fuck?" It seemed to be the five-million-dollar question of the moment.

The big hand waved again. "As I said, he did not take kindly to my insistence." Holding his arm up, gravity kept most of the blood in place. "It will heal soon enough."

Before I was aware she had even stood, Cassandra walked past me and up to Quintus. She didn't say anything, just stared at his wound. For a moment, I was afraid she was going to drink the blood, but that wasn't the look in her eye. I didn't know what it was, but it wasn't that.

She wrapped her long fingers around his wrist and the fingers of the other hand directly over the wound. Closing her eyes, she stood perfectly still for just a few moments. When she moved her hands, the wound was completely healed. Even a vampire's regular healing didn't work that fast on something that deep.

Cassandra had healed it. Somehow.

I stared at her.

Quintus stared at her.

She stared back, but was far less unsettled than the two of us.

No one said anything for what seemed like forever. When the utter silence was finally broken, it was Quintus's resounding voice that did it. "Another answer slides firmly into place."

I shook myself out of my surprise and looked at him. "What?"

He laughed, still in shock. "She is a healer. That is why they were all crowding around her—why they were drawn to her. They could sense it. I would surmise they had not an inkling of what they were sensing, but they could tell. Just as I could feel it, but the answer as to what that feeling is remains like a scent on the breeze."

Cassandra blinked at both of us. "What does that mean?"

Quintus took her hands in his, both disappearing into his paws, as he led her back to the couch. His dark eyes filled with wonder. "Have either of you learned of the occurrence where vampires are sometimes turned with certain... abilities?"

She shook her head. "Vampire one-oh-one hasn't covered that yet." She smiled bravely, though I could tell she was worried.

He gave her the same rough breakdown I'd been on the receiving end of. "Vampires can sometimes inherit abilities, such as hypnotism or animal calling, but then there are those that can heal wounds of body, mind, and soul. They can achieve incredible things, powerful things, but they are unbelievably rare."

"How rare?" she asked curiously.

"You are only the second I have heard of. In over six hundred years, I have only known two, and it's been centuries since I first met the other."

Her pretty eyes widened dramatically. "I had no idea," she breathed. "I mean, I had no idea I could do it at all until I saw how deeply you were hurt. I felt this pull inside me that I couldn't ignore, so I followed it." She glanced at me. "I felt it when you put your hand in the glass, but all I had to do then was pull the glass out."

Quintus kissed her hand. "It is a rare gift." He looked at me. "Protect her." He certainly didn't mince any words. "As she comes into her ability, other vampires will be more strongly drawn to it, like dry land in the middle of the ocean, and know it for what it is. She could be vulnerable. It's clear her gift is strong, and strong empathic skills accompany the healing. Until she can control them and shield herself, she will be easily overwhelmed and easily sensed." He turned back to her, perhaps realizing how rude it was to talk about her instead of to her. "I cannot believe that anyone would purposely bring you harm, but harm could happen when others cannot control what they do. I do not know much more of the ability, but I know it comes with vulnerabilities."

I nodded slowly. Nothing he said actually surprised me, and nothing he told me to do went against what I already felt. "I'll take care of her," I promised them both.

Cassandra seemed to have drifted off into thought, staring at the window on the other side of the room. It was a lot to take in, particularly since I couldn't imagine she'd recovered from the night before. From human to vampire to wonder-of-all-wonders healer in forty-eight hours. Anyone would be shell-shocked.

"You should go, before the others become too incensed,"

Quintus suggested. "As much as it pains me to say, the window would be easier."

"Right." I nodded, casting a concerned glance at Cassandra. "Will it always be like this? I mean, is she always going to have to duck other vampires?"

He shrugged his massive shoulders. "I cannot say, but as she learns how to control it and how to shield herself, I do not think it will always be a danger. While she's still growing into it, it could be considerable trouble with the unrestrained. Those in any sort of pain will seek her out, want her to heal and help them, whether she can or not. Others will just sense the serenity in her and want to have it for themselves."

Frowning, I nodded again. "Okay, we should go, then. Cassandra." She didn't seem to hear me at first, so I repeated her name. After a moment, she turned to look at me with large, blinking eyes. "We need to go."

"Oh. Right. Of course." She got to her feet. "I'm sorry you got hurt because of me." This to Quintus.

He waved that hand again. "Think nothing of it."

She leaned up on her toes and kissed his cheek before I helped her out the window. There wasn't anyone around that I could tell, so I hustled us to my car and we got the hell out of Dodge.

☾○☽

We stayed silent as we pulled out of the parking lot. I wasn't sure where we should go. Maybe it would be best just to go back to the apartment, but for some reason, I worried about that. Was it safe there? What about during the day? I needed some advice, so I called the office.

"Please tell me that you haven't turned another one, D," Sadie said. I quickly got the impression she was only half-joking.

"No," I replied. "But there's been a...development." I frowned, realizing I sounded like I was in a cop movie. "We were just down at Five, and something strange happened." I summarized for her quickly.

She didn't say anything for a few moments. "I've known some people who attracted weird shit, but you're just taking the fucking Oscar." She wasn't usually prone to swearing, so I knew I'd once again managed to catch her by surprise. There was another long pause I didn't feel right about filling, so I waited. "Okay, well, Quintus is right about how rare this is. I've only ever met one healer in nearly a century. You did right getting her out of there. I'd recommend taking her to the Coven House. There is someone there that might help, though she is...odd. She may or may not agree to help."

I reacted hard and unfavorably to that. My knee-jerk reaction blotted out that last sentence. "But that place is filled with fucking vampires. Won't we just face the same issues?"

"Think of it as a controlled setting. Vampires who join the coven tend to be more responsible and controlled than random crowds at vampire bars. And Jade, Adelheid's coven leader, governs well. She can't always control what her vamps do outside the Coven House, but no one dares break a rule *inside* it. Shayna, her chief warden, sees to that. They can help protect Cassandra while she learns, and Jade will have better access to the ancient texts that could help, if needed."

Thinking back to that scene at the bar, I still didn't like it, but what she said made sense. I also knew she knew more than I did about this. I had needed advice, and now I had it. If there was even a chance that someone there could help... "All right, tell me how to get there."

CHAPTER TWENTY-FOUR

My brain didn't really know how to process everything that had happened, so I tried to ignore whatever wasn't immediately important. Cassandra was becoming a super vampire. That's how I thought of it, because it just helped put it in some kind of perspective. And great power comes with great responsibility, so while she was learning to use her superpowers, I had to watch her back.

I could handle that, right? I would damn well find a way, because I couldn't let Cassandra down, too.

"D, I'm frightened," she said softly.

"I would be, too." I wasn't lying either. Becoming a vampire in the first place had kind of scared the...life out of me. (I couldn't help that one.) I couldn't imagine what would happen if someone told me I'd gotten crazy powers, too. "It's going to be okay, though. Sadie knows things, and she wouldn't steer us wrong. The people in charge at the Coven House should be able to help you learn how to handle whatever is coming your way. I promise. It will be all right." I gave her a brief sidelong smile.

She returned the smile, looking like she was trying to be as optimistic as possible when she was probably freaking the fuck out inside.

Turning her head, she peered out the window. I put all my attention into driving.

The Coven House was located in one of the more rural sections of Adelheid, away from the city center and deep in the forest. Sadie said they owned a huge piece of land and most of it surrounded the house on three sides. It was a private vampire sanctuary, of a sort, and had us driving down a rural road with old pavement and very tall trees rising on either side.

I drove around a curve, headlights swinging with me, coming around a clump of trees very near the edge. I could see very little of what was ahead until I was practically on top of it. What I remembered next were my high beams reflecting off the impossibly white skin and dress of a small figure…

…standing right in the middle of the damn road.

Slamming on the brakes still made me too late. Cassandra screamed as the front end of the car hit the figure, stopping just short of going *over* it, but it flew several feet ahead. Cassandra and I both sat frozen for an instant. It would have been one or two heartbeats, if our hearts still beat, before rushing out of the car. The scent of blood assaulted my sinuses the instant I caught the air.

Lying in the road was a fucking kid. She had to be maybe ten or eleven years old, thin and pale, with pale hair. It was pale beyond blonde. It was almost white, and it was covered in blood because her head was nearly severed from her neck, only held together by parts at the back. It was all white and red, like some modern art nightmare.

There was something…off about the body, but I couldn't register it at the time to know what I was looking at. All I could see was a dead kid and a dent in the front of my car.

"Oh my God," I gasped. I felt nauseous. I knew vampires couldn't throw up, but I still felt like hell. "We… We need to call the cops or something. She can't possibly be alive, can she? Oh, fucking hell, what did I do? I didn't even see her!" My brain spun too fast to catch.

Cassandra didn't say anything, just walked slowly toward the corpse. I watched her as I fumbled in my pocket for my cell and managed to drop it. As I picked it up, she put her hands on the girl's head. I was about to ask "what the fuck are you doing" but didn't get any further than "what" before I saw my answer.

The air tingled on my skin. I recognized it. It was magic. I felt like this whenever Sarah did her thing. The muscles and skin knit themselves together before my eyes, and the kid's head reattached. It's the only way to describe it.

"She's a vampire," Cassandra said softly. She wasn't even looking at me as she lifted her wrist to her lips and tore a vein open, holding it over the girl's partially open mouth. It dripped inside.

We waited. My cell phone felt like a rock in my hand as I stared, dumbfounded, at the scene before me.

The kid coughed and sat up sharply. Her eyes, nearly white as well, looked around wildly as she touched her neck and head. Pulling back her hands, she saw the blood but looked like she didn't believe it.

"What have you done?" she wailed suddenly, clutching her temples with the heels of her hands. "I almost had it that time, you idiots!"

Cassandra and I exchanged one very confused glance and then both turned back to the girl, who was pushing herself to her feet and dusting herself off.

"D," Cassandra breathed. "This girl is...ancient." Her eyes were so wide I feared they'd fall out.

"What?" It was like a joke I wasn't being let in on, and not a very funny one.

The little one scowled at us. "I'm an ancient. I'm over two thousand years old and I'm *done*!" She turned and stalked into the forest.

After all of this, I couldn't let that go and followed her. "What the hell are you talking about?"

She spun around. "How would you like to spend eternity

in the body of a ten-year-old? I've been trying to off myself for centuries, but apparently, the gods hate me, because it never works. I almost had it tonight, but here I am."

I gaped. "You mean you walked in front of my car *on purpose*!?"

"Yes."

Blinking, I shook my head. "You little bitch." I suddenly didn't care that she looked like a middle school kid. "You were going to let me carry that around on my conscience for the rest of my life?"

She seemed taken back by that, but for just a moment. "If you'd paid attention, you would have realized I was a vampire. If you had asked at the Coven House, they'd have told you what my deal was." She started walking again.

"That shit ain't right," I said, following again. "That's no excuse! My God, I didn't realize being alive for two thousand years made you the most inconsiderate, callous person on the face of the planet!"

"How outward thinking were *you* at ten?" She tossed her words disdainfully over her shoulder.

She had me there. Like many fifth graders, I hadn't been the most aware of the outside world, but... "You're not ten."

Stopping again, she turned to me. "Are you going to stop following me?"

I knew I should have—Cassandra was back at the car—but I couldn't make myself turn around just yet. I'd gone through a huge shock and thought I had killed a little girl, only to find out she'd pulled this stunt herself. That really pissed me off and I had been wound up before that, so I needed to do *something* with it. Yelling at her seemed like a good idea.

"I just can't believe you'd do that to someone," I finally said.

She pursed her lips. "If I apologize, will you go away?"

I crossed my arms. "Sure."

"I'm sorry."

Turning, she started stalking away again. I growled and returned to Cassandra.

"What the hell is going on?" she asked, clearly bewildered.

"I'll explain in the car."

Chapter Twenty-Five

"Can you imagine being trapped inside the body of a kid for two thousand years?" I asked as we started driving to the Coven House. I was still pissed, but the full impact of the concept had sunk in.

"No," she replied with a visible full-bodied shudder. "I'd rather not even imagine."

I sensed the deep darkness again and stopped talking. This didn't seem like the right time, so I kept driving.

In just a few minutes, we found the house and parked. A small white, blood-stained figure was just walking up the drive ahead of us. I started thinking that apparently this was just my *lucky night*.

We walked up behind her just as she reached the door. She didn't give us any notice as she opened it and went inside. There were two women in the hallway, which we could see straight into over her head.

The smaller of the two—an Asian woman with such smooth, perfect features she could have been a porcelain doll—looked the girl over from head to toe and then sighed dramatically. "What did you do *this* time, Albine?"

"Abby," the other replied petulantly, "and I would have made it if it hadn't been for the two idiots behind me." She stalked off to a door that, from the quick glimpse I got, looked like it went to a basement.

"We'd be the idiots," I introduced us. "I work for Sadie

Stanton. I'm not here on business, but she recommended we come."

The Asian woman nodded with a small smile. "She called and told me to expect you."

That was nice of her. "We didn't exactly expect it to be like this."

She gestured for us to come inside and walk into a sitting room, just off the right side of the hallway. It was opulently decorated, but not outside of taste. It reminded me of the backroom at 5, which wasn't really a plus. Inviting us to sit on the couch, she settled into the armchair across from it. The other woman in the hall took up a post at the doorway with her arms across her chest. She was an imposing figure.

"I'm Jade," the sitting one introduced herself. "You must be D and Cassandra. She told me a little of why you were coming." Her attention turned to Cassandra. "You must be our miraculous new vampire."

Vampires don't blush, but Cassandra came close. "This is what people keep telling me," she said, embarrassed.

"Please, be at ease. I can sense it on you, but you are safe here." Jade smiled again and gestured to the intimidating woman in the door. "This is Shayna Harel. She is our chief warden. No one in this house is unsafe under her watch. Believe me, her former life well qualifies her for it."

"What did you do?" I looked at her, various governmental acronyms and Jason Bourne movies flashing through my mind.

She smirked. "I would tell you," she said with a faint accent, maybe Middle Eastern, "but then I would have to kill you."

I knew it was an old line, but from *her*, I believed it. "Forget I asked."

"I apologize for Abby," Jade was saying. "She is… troubled, but she can be of use to you. She was turned with some healing abilities, and vampires grow more powerful as they age, so she can help. She will be able to teach you to build mental and emotional defenses, so you will be able to more easily mix with the world and with less restrained vampires without worry."

Now I knew what Sadie had meant by 'odd' when she referenced someone who could help at the house.

Cassandra bit her bottom lip. "I don't really have that much trouble around people," she protested softly.

Jade nodded knowingly. "But it's getting a little harder now than it used to be, isn't it?"

"A little," Cassandra conceded, "but I didn't think much of it."

"Power like this grows as you acclimate to your new life. If you learn how to shield yourself now, you will be much better off in the long run. Abby can help you with that," the coven leader explained.

"If she sticks around long enough," I mumbled before I could stop myself.

Jade didn't look upset, but neither did she look amused. "Abby will help. She may not seem like it, but she has a good heart. She simply falls into these episodes from time to time, lamenting the way her life has gone. No one knows why she remains alive. It is like fate, or whatever god you may believe in, has a hand in it. She is meant to be here, but now that this episode is over with, she will be more cooperative and will understand the necessity. You may rely on her."

Again, I conceded to the one who would know better than I, but I didn't like it any better than before. "Until she gets over the bad mood, she may not be too happy with Cassandra. She healed her."

Jade's curious expression prompted Cassandra to tell the story. The woman looked impressed. "That is considerable power in one so young." She examined Cassandra for a few moments more before turning to me. "I believe I am to understand she is living with you?"

I felt embarrassed, although I didn't know why. I nodded.

"A wise precaution with a new vampire," she said as she turned back to Cassandra. "I would, however, now recommend you stay here for a few nights to take advantage of the safety of the Coven House and Abby's assistance."

"Is that really necessary?" I asked, but even as I said it, I could see the wisdom. I was certain they had defenses in place for the daylight hours that I didn't have. I held up a hand. "Yeah, I guess it's a good idea. What about me? Should I...stay too?" I felt weird asking.

Jade shrugged in a small gesture. "You are welcome to, if you wish. Perhaps you may consider allowing Cassandra a night or two on her own, however, to be assured she can handle herself alone as she learns her new powers."

To make sure I didn't help too much or get used as a crutch, she meant, but she had managed to say it very politely. She was a diplomat. I didn't like it, but it wasn't really up to me. I turned to Cassandra. "What do you think?" She didn't reply right away, so I said her name.

Now she turned to me, blinking, and then nodded. "It is perhaps wise to stay here while I learn." She smiled and put her hand over mine. "I'll be all right on my own. I'm sure Ms. Harel here will see to my safety adequately."

I risked a glance at the woman before turning to Cassandra with a nod. "If you're sure," I said. "At least we have your stuff in the car still." I smiled slightly and then looked at my phone. "Unfortunately, I have an appointment soon so I'm going to have to go. I'll help get some of your stuff inside first and take the rest back to my place." After all, she wasn't going to be living here permanently.

She nodded. "I'll help."

We walked outside together. Now that we weren't be observed, I looked at her again. "Are you sure you're okay with this?"

"I get a good feeling from Jade," she said with a nod. "Now I know these feelings are real indicators. I don't know much about these skills I'm going to be acquiring, but I'd like to learn all I can. This seems like the place to do it."

"You know where I am if you need me." I smiled as we reached the car.

She smiled back and kissed my cheek. "Thank you."

CHAPTER TWENTY-SIX

I went straight to the office.

The further away from the Coven House I got, the more unsettled I felt about the whole thing. I didn't know Jade or Shayna, and that Abby kid was a psychotic little bitch, so why was I leaving Cassandra with them? Once I thought that, I had to remind myself that Sadie had said it would be okay and that this was the town's coven. They knew their shit better than I did. I had to remind myself of these things more forcibly as I went, but eventually, I got the idea enough to stop dwelling. Mostly.

When I walked inside, I found Dakota sitting on the couch in the front office and Sadie leaning back against Madison's desk. Sadie looked at me.

"D..." She sounded surprised. "I wasn't sure if I would see you in here tonight. I told Sarah you might not be and to get in touch with you."

I grunted. "She hasn't yet, but I wouldn't leave her on her own. Besides, Jade suggested Cassandra stay there so she could work with Abby. Apparently, the little freak is older than the earth and can help her set up psychic defenses or something."

"Who?"

"Abby," I explained. "She's this vampire who is something like two thousand years old in the body of a ten-year-old."

Sadie shuddered. "Oh, right. Her. She creeps me out.

Jade always refers to her as Albine, so I didn't know who you meant at first."

"I could have used knowing about her a few months ago." Dakota snorted, not looking up from the clipboard she had on her knees.

"You didn't ask," Sadie said.

I glanced her way. "Where's your shadow?"

Dakota lifted her eyes and gave me a withering look. They were pale brown today, but prone to changing. "He's off looking for his inner child or some shit. Don't worry. He's promised I won't be without him for long." Her gaze dropped back to her paperwork. "Jerk leaves me on my own in the woods for two hundred years and then thinks I need a big brother. I'm four hundred fucking years old. I think I can manage on my own."

"Oh, I don't know about that." This was from Sadie. "We need someone around here to keep you in line."

Dakota hissed without bothering to look up. She did some shifter voodoo in her throat and perfectly replicated an angry snake. "I don't really like you that much, you know."

My boss chuckled. "Then what are you doing here? I'm pretty sure you can fill out paperwork at your apartment."

The hunter looked around shiftily and even I could tell that Sadie had caught her. "I'm hiding, okay? Eddie thinks I'm home."

"I thought he hated when you called him Eddie."

"He does."

Sadie tilted her head curiously. "Why aren't you hiding at your girlfriend's, then?"

The theriomorph didn't blush, but she did look almost sheepish. "If you must know, she's in Boston visiting her parents. We agreed they aren't ready to meet me yet."

"You are kind of frightening."

I hadn't seen Dakota's girlfriend, because she was a cop in Hartford—about an hour away from Adelheid—but according to the others, she was a looker and didn't take any crap from Dakota. Being male, sue me, I could appreciate the idea of two women, but not as much as I might have if one of them didn't kind of scare me. I'll admit it. Dakota could be kind of frightening. Sadie was right about that.

Their interplay helped distract me from the dwelling I was trying not to do, but I noticed that Madison had been suspiciously quiet. A little more distraction couldn't hurt, so I walked behind the desk and left Sadie and Dakota to their bickering.

I paused behind her chair, and she glanced up at me with a friendly smile. "I assume Sarah's appointment is still on for tonight?" I asked. "I haven't heard from her, so I guess she just plans to wing it."

She nodded. "She should be in at any time now." Her eyes ran up and down my face and then added, "You look tired."

"It's been a hell of a couple of days."

"I've heard." She turned back to her computer, but the smart phone next to her keyboard buzzed. She picked it up, looked at it, and then smiled privately but set it away without replying.

I couldn't help myself. "Boyfriend?"

Madison glanced at me in a way I can only describe as coy. "Of a sort."

Of course, that was just the sort of answer I'd want to follow up on, but I didn't get the chance because Sarah walked in. She saw how many people were in the front office and chuckled. "I didn't realize I was showing up for a party."

"It was very last minute," Sadie offered dryly.

It was then that I realized I was the only guy in a room with four women. That could either be very, very good or very, very bad. Before it got a chance to go from the former to the latter, I asked Sarah, "Are we ready to go?"

She nodded, and I followed her out. There was a quiet chorus of farewells behind us, but Sadie and Dakota had already started up again before the door was even shut.

"Are they really always like that?" I asked as we got into the car. Since that first appointment, I'd convinced her to let me start driving. It felt more...bodyguard-like.

She chuckled as I started the engine. "Often enough, but they really do care about each other. I'm not in the office as much as some, but I can see it. I know a little about the pair of them. Sadie never had any siblings, and Dakota lost most of hers in some way or another over the centuries. I think they fill the gap with each other, and Madison as their little sister."

I smirked. "I can see that. I wonder how Madison feels about being the little sister."

"I don't see how she has much choice." Sarah shrugged. "She's by far the youngest, and her own older brother died a couple of years ago."

Oh yeah, I'd heard about that. Madison's brother Cameron was the guy who started the ball rolling on the law, the Preternatural Rights Act of 2010, and he was murdered just days before the president signed it. Sadie had been his girl and almost got killed herself the same night. If she hadn't been the "poster girl" before that, she certainly was after it.

"I kind of like listening to them," I admitted. "They're funny when they get all...like that."

"Yeah, they are. I wouldn't say it to them, though. They might seem cute when they're cats and dogs with each other, but never forget all three of them could probably eat you for breakfast." She grinned.

It was a disturbing thought, but at least I was feeling a little better about the evening.

Chapter Twenty-Seven

After we finished our appointments, which didn't have more than the usual trouble because apparently I was scary to look at, I spent a little time in the office to fix a computer problem for Madison and then went home.

I found the quiet of my apartment suddenly disconcerting. Cassandra had only been there one night, but her presence had made an impact on my mood. I didn't like the place now. Jade had recommended I not stay at the Coven House, so I would resist my unhappiness. That didn't stop me from making a quick call, but Cassandra assured me all was well.

With little else to do and a lot of anxious energy to burn, I sat down and played *World of Warcraft* for a while. I found it hard to focus, though, so I logged off and lay on the couch instead. Vampires don't nap, so I kind of just meditated, in a totally unguided and not-really-trying kind of way. Okay, I stared at the ceiling and dwelled.

I didn't fall asleep. Vampires don't do that. We don't sleep like normal people anymore, even if we try, but I kind of drifted off. I guess you could call it a daydream, although it didn't have that whimsical feel. It was more like a sleeping dream and yet not.

I really can't explain it.

Whatever it was, I was in the middle of it. I was at 5, but in the parking lot, and the air was gray, like in the hours just before sunrise. It was the sort of surreal dimness I no longer saw firsthand but simply felt just before the sun swept me under. A breeze was blowing and stirring the trees across the street, but it looked almost in slow motion. I felt like I was in a bad Western movie.

Cielle stood in front of me. Her exotic features were distorted in frustration and fear as her mouth moved, trying to say something, but no sound came out. In fact, there was no sound anywhere. It was a silent movie. Cielle pleaded with me, but I couldn't understand her. I took her hands in mine as she gestured frantically, but still nothing.

Behind her, I watched a vague shadowy figure approaching. I tried to warn her, but I couldn't make any sound either. I couldn't move. Once the figure began its approach, I was frozen in place and forced to watch as the figure stalked up. Cielle never turned to face it. The figure swung a long blade and cut off her head. I shouted soundlessly as it rolled away and her body crumbled, taking me with her because my hands were stuck to hers…

I 'woke' with a gasp, if that's the appropriate verb for it. If I'd still had a beating heart, I was sure it would have been pounding. In fact, for a moment I thought it had started beating again, until I realized the sound was someone knocking on my door.

Putting my hand on my chest, I got off the couch and answered the door. I kind of hoped it would be Cassandra, but it wasn't.

It was my ex.

"Fuck, what do you want now?" I sighed. I was beyond 'not in the mood' to deal with her right now, so I didn't care too much about subtlety or manners. Granted, I'm not sure I had much use for either before that. I could also feel dawn very close and knew I didn't have much time for her shit.

She shifted her feet, looking briefly uncomfortable before that smile returned. It was the same expression she had on her face last time, but this time, it looked strained.

Maybe it was just the hour. The hour before dawn seemed to be a rough one for any species.

Raven shrugged. At least she was wearing less make-up now. She was actually kind of pretty, when she didn't have all that crap painted on her face. "I thought maybe you'd be feeling a little differently than the other night. I'm sorry I got so pushy, but I really miss you, D."

Frowning, I didn't think this sounded anything like her. Could dawn be forcing a moment of true honesty? It seemed unlikely, but then, stranger things had happened. "Forget about it," I said uncomfortably. Dawn was coming fast now, and it made my head fill with fog. It didn't usually, but I wasn't usually trying to fight it like I had to now. "I can't say that I feel any different, though."

The fog thickened, and I sighed, scrubbing my hands over my eyes. Then there seemed to be a faint buzzing, which was new. I made a mental note to never fight against dawn. It would always win, which I had already known.

She tilted her head, black hair falling to one side as she looked up at me. "Are you sure you don't even miss me a little?"

I guessed I couldn't really say that. When she looked at me like that, I couldn't help but think of the few good moments there had been, and there had been some. I smiled a little and shrugged with one shoulder. "Maybe a little, sometimes, you know," I confessed. The buzzing faded slightly, but everything was still foggy. I'd have to lie down soon. "But that doesn't change anything, Rave. I'm sorry, but it's over between us, and it's going to stay that way."

She pouted, actually pouted, straightening up and stepping into me, resting her hands on my chest. I inhaled deeply and caught the scent of her whatever-flower shampoo she used and her perfume, and it flooded what spaces were left free in my head in a way that had never happened before. I lifted my head and forcibly stopped breathing. Blinking, I tried to clear my mind of a few memories that slipped in. The good memories.

In the back of my mind, my old friend—the black hole of hungry restlessness—began to stir again. It had been quiet lately, but the close dawn and the memories of Raven at the front of my mind brought it back. It drew me toward her.

Somehow, she seemed to know and leaned in more, lifted her head. I stared down at her mouth, heard her heart beating hard and breath coming rapidly. For a moment, I was tempted…

Then I saw the bandage on her neck. The buzzing and fog cleared in an instant. I didn't really know what made it come to mind, but something forced it to the surface. I remembered slipping on blood, Cassandra and the open door, the broken jar and the blood on her chin. Could it have been an attack and not an accident? It seemed more probable, now that I thought of it.

Pieces of a theory clicked. Raven might still have a key. She opened the door while I was out. Cassandra was walking by the door. Spooked, they argued, and Raven got angry and maybe took a swing. Cassandra would fight back the way a new vampire would: with teeth to the throat. And then maybe fell and hit her head, or she blanked out because it was a startling thing to do. The vampire could just come out of nowhere.

The bandage in the right biting place on the neck seemed to suggest it, and I could imagine Raven doing it. Rage, just barely controlled, surged through my now-clear mind. I didn't care I had no proof. The idea was enough.

I looked down into her eyes, burying the rage I felt with a dark smile. "Get. The fuck. Out. Of here." I pointed down the hall.

Her eyes widened at my sudden reversal, but too bad for her. I put my hand on her shoulder and steered her back into the hall.

"Go!"

She seemed to know I was serious and hurried away with only a couple of looks back. I thought I saw someone else, further down the hall, but they were gone before I could get a good look. Maybe it had been no one at all.

Shaking myself and feeling miserable for what I'd almost done with the ex I again remembered I didn't like, I went back in my apartment and shut the door. Feeling a little weird about things suddenly, I grabbed the small table crammed in the corner that served as a dining room and flipped it on its side like a barricade, jamming it in front of the door.

I hit the couch just before dawn took over.

Chapter Twenty-Eight

Despite the previous night's paranoia, I awoke in one piece. All in all, that was a good thing. The table hadn't been moved, so I doubted anyone had tried to get in. I felt like hell, though. Fragmentary images floated around in my mind, the way a dream you're forgetting does right after waking, but I'd never dreamed as a vampire and didn't think vampires could during the day.

I couldn't grab onto any of them enough to figure it out. Otherwise, I kind of just felt like I'd been beaten up, and I didn't know what that was all about. The coma wasn't like sleep. It didn't change the way sleep could, but that's what it felt like. It felt like I was waking up from a bad night's sleep.

Trying to shrug it off, I got up and finally took that shower. I got dressed in clean clothes but realized they were among the last ones I had. Laundry would need doing, but I didn't look forward to the all-night laundry mat. Creepy people were there.

Next, I had breakfast and then some time at the computer. I called the Coven House and got chastised by Harel for being a 'mother hen,' which sounded funny in her accent, and was then told Cassandra was busy. I went on WoW and killed some elementals to take out my annoyance with the warden. I considered making a new character that looked like her just to let it be killed by kobolds, but then I thought that would be too spiteful.

I was just heading out to the office when my cell phone

rang. It was Quintus.

"I just received a disturbing call," he said without any preamble, but then he paused. That of course was just damned annoying, and it wasn't like I was brimming with patience in the first place. I was just about to say something when he went on, sounding uncertain about what he was saying, "It sounded like Cassandra, at first, but she did not sound like herself. I then realized it was not her. It was a woman, but every word from her was a struggle."

"What?" I was quite the probing investigator.

"D, I am not sure how, but…I think it was Cielle."

Dead silence on my end. This old fuck had obviously been out in the daylight and made himself stupid crazy.

"Look, old man, have you been hitting the special blood or something?"

"I know, I know," he said quickly. "Hear me out before you make the call to the vampires in the clean white coats." He paused and when I didn't object, he continued, "I listened to her speak, and her voice had the same inflections as Cielle. It was not just that, but also what she said. And that is the reason I am calling you. She told me she could not reach you, but she wanted you to know that she is still here and that he has her power."

I really had no idea what to say to that. I stood outside my apartment, gaping like a fish in the bottom of a boat while my brain desperately tried to process.

"Are you still there, D?"

"Yeah, yeah, I'm still here." I snapped out of my stupor. "I mean… What? Where the hell did you get this?"

"She said, and I quote, 'Tell D I couldn't reach him. Tell him that he has my powers.'"

"That I have her powers? What powers? What the hell?" I repeated.

Quintus paused. "I do not think she meant you. That

was all that was said, but 'he' was emphasized in a way that made me believe she meant this man that meant her harm. This is only my intuition, but it has been unerring for many years."

He was older and wiser, the bastard. That had to be worth something, but it didn't mean that any of this made sense.

"I don't suppose you have any other insights?" I finally asked.

"I am afraid not, my friend. I am as perplexed as you are."

I sighed. "Well, that fucking figures."

☾○☽

I went into the office. This time, everyone was apparently working, for a change, so I just waited until Sarah showed up. I'd been thinking about something I wanted to ask her since I got off the phone with Quintus, but I waited till we were on the road.

"Can I ask you a question?"

"You just did." She eyed me sidelong, but she smiled. "But go ahead."

I considered my words. "Can you animate a dead—I mean ultra-dead—vampire?"

From her expression, I guessed she hadn't been expecting that. "That depends on a few things," she answered while I turned right onto Sherwood Street. "Animating vampires isn't like animating humans or even shifters. How old was this vamp when they died?"

Come to think of it, I wasn't sure. "A few hundred years, but I don't know what her exact age was."

"How long has she been second dead?"

Second dead, that was a good way of putting it. "A couple of weeks."

She shook her head. "I'm sorry, but that's a no-go." She paused thoughtfully. "Animating is an odd piece of sorcery. If you believe in an afterlife, and I do, then you believe that the body has a soul that departs at death and goes to the afterlife. When an animator brings someone back, for that short time, what are we bringing back? The personality is, mostly, there. The resurrected body seems to have the same feelings and connections, more strongly the closer to their time of death." She paused again. "With me so far?"

I nodded.

"It's the common belief of my kind that the soul and the mind have left residual traces in the body, and it's those traces we use to bring them back. These fade with time, so the older a corpse, the less of that person that's there when the body is animated. Also, less of the body is there, so talking gets harder when the muscles of the jaw and the tongue start rotting. I could raise a skeleton, but they wouldn't be able to talk. Anyway, I'm getting off topic. It's different with vampires. For some reason, those residual traces don't last as long. Maybe it's something about being dead for so long already. When they're second dead and the magic that brought them into their vampire state goes away, it takes the residual traces with it and leaves them as they would have been if they'd been really dead for all that time. I can raise a vampire if it's within a few days, there's some kind of delay or something, but after that, there's nothing I can do."

I sighed. It was a long-winded answer for what I had thought was a simple question, but I supposed that the information was good to have. "It's all right. It was a long shot anyway."

After a moment, she added. "I've heard some rumors about vampire deaths. I've heard a necromancer can pull a vamp up from longer dead than an animator, but I've never seen it. I've also heard that the spirits of dead vampires..." She paused, frowning as I parked in front of tonight's graveyard. "I don't know if this will matter to you, but since we're on the subject, sometimes a vampire's spirit can get trapped, without their body, on earth. I guess you could call it a vampire ghost."

That was a terrifying thought. "Why would that happen? Does it happen to all vampires when they die?" My first thought was: please, for the love of God, may that not happen to me. The second was: was that what the 'she' on the phone meant by "I'm still here"?

She shrugged. "I don't know. I don't know if it's true it happens at all. Like I said, it's a rumor, though I've heard they can take over the bodies of other vampires, if the mind is susceptible."

"That's a nasty thought." I got out of the car when she did, and tried not to think too hard about this, because I'd probably just end up freaking myself out.

Being a vampire had just gotten creepier since my turning, not less.

CHAPTER TWENTY-NINE

I thought about what Quintus and Sarah had said while I was ushering a pair of teenage protestors away, in the car on the way back to the office, and in my car as I left.

After all that thinking, you would presume I'd have things figured out. I didn't, but I had some theories. If Sarah was right about vampire ghosts wandering around, then Quintus might have been right about Cielle calling him. She might have somehow gotten a hold of someone's body and talked to him. She and I had never exchanged numbers before exchanging fluids, so she'd have no way to find me if she was working with limited resources. But then she had come to my apartment... Maybe she hadn't found the number at the same time? Seemed stupid, but not impossible. Quintus had said it sounded like she was struggling. Possession probably took a lot out of a ghost.

If this was true, then she was sending me a message, but why? Did the attack on me outside the office have something to do with her? I didn't know, but she said that she was still here and that could corroborate the ghost thing. If she was warning me about someone, like the guy that killed her, the message about "he" would be about that and it meant he had the same powers as she did.

What powers were those? I knew some vampires turned with special abilities other vampires didn't have, like Cassandra, but I realized that I didn't know what Cielle's had been.

Should I have thought of all of this sooner? Sure, but no one had ever accused me of being overly intelligent.

The one person who would know was the one I went to. As I pulled into the parking lot, I began to think about just renting a room at the place.

"What powers did Cielle have?" I asked as soon as I reached the bar and got the big man's attention.

"Good evening to you too," he replied, setting down a glass.

I paused. "Good evening. What powers did Cielle have?"

He frowned and tilted his head. "You were not aware?"

"No."

"She was what mythology would call a succubus." He smirked slightly, drying another glass and setting it on the display behind the bar. "She was capable of manipulating sexual energies, desires. In a human, she could coerce the weaker-willed into doing as she desired. Men and women alike responded to her powers, which gave her quite an advantage, as vampires go. The details themselves are open to conjecture. I would surmise a cognitively aware or perceptive person could tell when they were being manipulated. They may even be able to resist her, to a degree, though with her age, they would still feel and perhaps respond to the compulsion."

I frowned and wondered if I should feel like a puppet. "Did she do that to me?"

He shook his head. "No. You resisted."

"I resisted?"

"You resisted. She confided to me that she attempted to compel you, and it began to take hold, but that you 'dug your mental heels in,' and she failed to draw you further." He chuckled. "In case you were concerned, what occurred between the two of you was pure and honest sexual chemistry with no manipulation on either part. It was your high resistance that attracted her more. She said it was like you had your own power, a power to resist others' abilities, which she'd heard of but never seen. So, that shows how rare it was for her to find someone who can so firmly resist her outright." He paused, mirth fleeing his eyes. "It was rare that someone *could*," he amended quietly.

I thought about that and tried not to feel guilty. "She said that 'he has my powers,' right?" He nodded. The hard drive in my brain whirred loudly as it processed what he had said and what little I knew. I was trying to put pieces together. "Could that be why she wanted me to help her, because I could resist this guy's powers? That maybe I have some actual ability to do that?"

Now it was Quintus's turn to look thoughtful. "That would be my conclusion, though it does not explain why she could not fend him off on her own. She was not a young vampire and was strong in her own right. I would have considered it an even match, unless this mysterious assailant was much older and more powerful."

"I don't have the answer to that one." I sighed, still thinking. "Why did she have to do it that way, Quintus?" I finally asked, rubbing the back of my neck. I still didn't understand it. "She could have just asked me, but she pissed me off so bad, I didn't want anything to do with her. Now she's dead."

"She did not always fully understand the feelings of others. I am certain she was afraid you'd say no, so she turned you and hoped for the best. Perhaps she hoped that once you were a vampire, you would in turn need her." He shrugged his massive shoulders.

I tapped my fingers on the bar. I didn't want to say that her getting murdered was her own fault, but it kind of was. If she had asked me, what would I have said? I didn't know if I would have listened, but maybe I would have. I just wished she had given me the chance first. If she had, maybe things would have turned out differently, and maybe she wouldn't be dead. There was no way to know.

"Beaumont told me that sometimes a vampire dies—you know, for good—and their spirit gets stuck on earth. They just wander around like a ghost forever, maybe eventually getting lucky and finding someone to possess." I was still bothered by the idea.

"I have heard that." He nodded again. "It is why I considered that I was talking to Cielle, though it is still disconcerting to think so. I cannot say I have ever met someone who was…possessed."

I shuddered. "I hope it doesn't happen very often." Pause. "I hope it didn't happen to Cielle. I mean, I hated her for what she did, but I wouldn't wish that on her. When you're dead for good, you should be dead for good."

Quintus folded his arms across his chest. "Perhaps it is as it is with human ghosts," he suggested. "Trapped here because of something particular and can be released, or helped along, by the right person."

Thinking about that, I hoped that was true for all ghosts. "It's a good thought, and I hope so. I'm just not sure if I should try to do something. Can you hold a séance for a vampire ghost? Can I talk to her, or find out if it's even true?"

"That, I do not know any more than you do. For now, I would think on things. And watch your back. If her murderer is after you, you should be on your guard. You may be resistant, but you're not immortal." He set a glass down on the bar in front of me and poured some blood into it.

"Thanks," I said quietly, pulling it toward me.

I sat there for a little while, kind of wallowing in the torment and tumult of my own thoughts. Words like 'ghost' and 'séance' came up a lot. I even thought about calling those guys on television, the ones that chased ghosts around, but then decided that with all the creepy crawly characters out there these days, they probably had their hands full.

After finishing my glass, I headed out. The air was clear and warm, and I took a breath just because I could. Maybe it made me feel a little human again, just for a moment. I even looked around, just in case that jerk was lingering, but I didn't see anyone, so I headed to my car. My mind wasn't any quieter than it had been inside, but if I sat at that bar too long, I'd either turn into a cliché or a sitcom character. I elected to leave instead.

There was only one place I was going to go now, though. I had to see Cassandra, and I also wanted to talk to Jade.

Chapter Thirty

Cassandra was again busy with Abby when I arrived, but I was assured they'd be done soon. Jade offered to sit with me. She even agreed to answer some of my questions, if she could. I guessed she would be a good source for all things vampire, right?

I didn't really know how to start, as we sat in her office.

"I feel really strange asking this, but how much do you know about...succubi?" I winced even as I asked.

She chuckled, but it didn't sound like it was *at* me, precisely. "I don't really like to use that term, because it's inaccurate. We don't precisely have a succinct term for what it is, which is why so many still use the old name." Brushing a long strand of black hair behind her ear, she went on. "There isn't a lot to know, however. All people are naturally able to manipulate the emotions of others. Some are better at it. The vampires with this ability are especially able to manipulate desire, to make you want to do something. Generally, it's whatever they're telling you to do. They make you want to do it. It's related to sexual desire, but it isn't always about that."

I nodded slowly. "What about if someone was able to resist that manipulation?"

Jade cocked her head to one side, one corner of her mouth tilted upward curiously. "Many people are able to resist in some degree. The stronger impulse control a person has, the better able they are to curb their desires. However, someone who is able to resist completely, even when the full strength of the vampire's powers is being used, is rare." She paused. "D, why are you asking me about this? You don't have this ability."

That surprised me. "You can tell?"

She nodded. "You need to know these sorts of things if you're going to lead a coven."

I supposed that made sense. Vampires still knew too much. "It's about the one who turned me. She's dead now, but she had this power." I stopped and tried to figure out how much I should actually say. It felt kind of personal.

"I suppose you're the one who was able to resist it?" she asked.

"Yeah," I admitted. "I'm just curious how it worked. It was suggested that maybe I have my own power, one that lets me resist magic like that?" I felt crazy as I said it, but then, I was a vampire now. I guess I was already stretching that boundary.

"I've heard of such powers but have never seen it," Jade said thoughtfully.

Anything else we had been planning to ask was cut short by the sound of shattering glass and a scream. It sounded like Cassandra. Every nerve stood on end. I shared the briefest look with Jade before we bolted out of the office, rushing down the long hall toward the source of the noise.

Shayna nearly leapt over our heads to get there, and Abby was just dashing up the stairs as we passed.

"What happened?" she asked, but no one stopped to answer.

In a bedroom in the back, we found Cassandra sitting on the floor. The window beside her was broken, glass all over the floor, and she looked dazed.

I was at her side in an instant. "What happened?" I asked, but the others all asked the same thing just a second behind me. She didn't answer, or even look at me. I put my hands gently on her face and tilted it to meet mine. The look in those pale eyes was distant. I don't know how to explain it, exactly, but she wasn't with us. It took a moment before she came into herself, blinking and looking around.

"What?" she asked.

"Cassandra," I said gently, "What happened?"

She looked at the window. "I was sitting in the chair." Glancing over her shoulder, she frowned when she seemed to realize she was on the floor. "Abby had gone into the basement. I felt odd for a moment, like my head was kind of foggy, but we have been learning a lot. She's been teaching me mental shields, and it gives me headaches." She smiled sheepishly, but it faded fast. "I heard the window break, and a man started to climb in. I screamed…and then I don't remember what happened. Maybe he hit me."

"Where is he now?" Shayna asked, sniffing the air like an attack German Shepherd or something. Her eyes darted around the room.

"I don't know."

I looked her over, trying to see if there was any evidence that she'd been hit. I had to imagine even vampires didn't do well with repeated concussions. "Where the hell were you?" I snapped over my shoulder, making a point of glaring at Shayna. Worry for Cassandra and anger at not being here, again, when something happened to her fueled my anger with the warden. "You said she'd be safe here!"

Shayna didn't reply right away. Her face was impassive, but I thought I sensed embarrassment. "It *is* safe here," she replied tightly. "I don't know how anyone could've gotten past my wardens and the spell wards on the windows." She hissed. "He must be gone now, though. I don't smell anyone unfamiliar."

I turned my body slightly, meeting her gaze. "Don't you think you should, I don't know, go out and check? I mean, it's hardly my job, but even I know this shit."

"Don't tell me my job, youngling," she snapped. "This is unprecedented."

"Well, maybe you're just not very good at what you do." It was out of my mouth before I could stop it.

She stepped forward. "Shut your mouth or I'll shut it for you."

Before either of us could get to exchanging blows, or Jade could tell the kids to behave, another voice cut through us.

"Leave him the hell alone!"

At first, I didn't know who had said it. It sounded almost masculine, although young, but I was the only man in the room. Then I turned and saw Cassandra. Her eyes were fully focused now...and *pissed*. The muscles in her shoulders were visibly bunched, like she was ready to jump up and start beating on somebody—no, specifically on Shayna. She was glaring straight past me.

She was defending me.

Even Harel looked taken back. She didn't have anything to say.

"Cassandra, it's all right," I said softly, forcing my ego and my anger back down where they belonged.

Her head whipped around and looked at me, but when she met my eyes, the anger faded. "What?" she asked, sounding like herself again.

I put my hand on her shoulder, which wasn't tense anymore. "It's all right. I'm sorry Shayna and I got a little short with each other. We're just worried."

Cassandra's gaze swung between me and the warden for an uncertain moment. I wondered if she didn't believe us, but then she nodded. "Okay."

"Let's move into another room," Jade suggested,

interjecting smoothly, "and let our warden do her job."

"That's a good idea." I nodded and got to my feet, offering a hand to Cassandra to help her up. We walked out and left Shayna to work, still looking a little shocked at Cassandra's reaction but saved from any more of my scathing (and useless) commentary.

CHAPTER THIRTY-ONE

Back in Jade's office, Cassandra sat on the sofa beside me and kept my hand inside both of hers. I had to resist the urge to put my arm around her shoulders. Jade excused herself, leaving us alone for a few minutes.

"Are you feeling okay?" I asked.

"Yeah." She nodded. "I'm just feeling a little dazed."

I glanced at her temple and over her hair again, just making sure there weren't any signs of a more serious injury. Head injuries were funny that way, but aside from the forgetting, she didn't seem too bad off. "That's understandable, but it's been all right here, besides that?"

She smiled faintly and nodded. "Oh yes. Abby is actually very nice, when you get used to her. She's been teaching me a lot. I feel like I'll be better able to handle things, on my own."

"That's good," I said out loud, even though inwardly I wanted to tell her that she wouldn't have to do things on her own. I didn't say it, though, because I knew a person couldn't always be counted on. You had to be able to stand on your own, too. "It's not too weird being here?"

"I'll have you know, D," Jade said as she swept back into the room, "that this happens to be a perfectly normal communal home. It just happens to lack heartbeats, regular food, and sunlight."

I laughed sheepishly. "Sorry."

She sat down. "It's all right." Her eyes swung to

Cassandra. "Have you remembered anything more about the breaking glass?" she asked. "Perhaps do you recall what this man looked like?"

"I remember a little," she replied, brows knitting in thought. "I couldn't tell how tall he was as he came through the window, but he was skinny. He had short dark hair and a thin nose." She traced her own nose with the tip of her finger. "I think he had dark eyes, kind of far apart. I remember thinking, briefly and kind of stupidly now, that he looked like a deer."

I frowned. The details she described were starting to sound very familiar, and I had flashes back to the attack outside the office, but before I could say so, Shayna beat me to it.

"That sounds like a guy who came by the Coven House a few weeks ago," she said, standing in the doorway. She looked at Jade. "There's no sign of him, and the wardens in that area have no idea how he got past them. It stinks of magic, though. I think someone should go out and investigate what might have done it. I'm not quite that good." She swung her gaze back to me. "There was a guy looking for a woman, a vampire, named Cielle. I had to tell him I didn't know anyone named that."

It shouldn't have surprised me, given everything, but it did. I felt every muscle in my body tense. Cassandra frowned and looked at me. "What's wrong?"

I inhaled slowly. "I think the guy who tried to break in here is the guy who killed the woman who turned me."

That got everyone's attention.

I spent the next few minutes explaining the story I had managed to avoid telling just a little while earlier. It didn't amount to much, however, because no one knew anything more than I did. Neither Jade nor Shayna had known Cielle or the guy who was after her, and none of us could guess why he might break into the Coven House, unless he thought I was there. And I still didn't know what his beef with me was, unless he just hated me because of Cielle.

Shayna came over to talk to Cassandra about some extra precautions that coven vamps were going to be advised of until they figured out how the guy got past their security. I wanted to listen in, but Abby came into the doorway and gestured for me to come over. I still didn't like her, but she was being nice to Cassandra, so I figured I would tolerate her.

"What's up?" I asked, trying to think of why she would want to talk to me.

"What's her story?" she asked, nodding at the blonde on the couch.

I appreciated the straightforward approach but was still surprised by the question. "Why are you asking me? Why don't you just ask her?"

She glanced past me briefly. "I have, but she doesn't like to talk about it. I get that, but sometimes it's almost like she doesn't want to talk because she doesn't know."

I frowned. "Like, she's got amnesia or something?" It sounded kind of ridiculous, because it obviously wasn't that. She'd taken me to her house with her stuff, unless she was the world's strangest thief.

"No." Abby shook her head slowly, uncertainly. "She's nice, but kind of odd."

My brows shot up. "This, coming from you?"

She looked at me dryly. "Consider the source, then. I know what I'm talking about." She paused. When she did, she was perfectly still and reminded me of a life-sized doll. Creepy as fuck. "There's been a couple times when she kind of faded out a little and then when I got her attention and started instructing her again, she almost seemed not to believe she was a vampire."

"That's odd." I winced on the inside when I echoed her words, for no particular reason. "Sadie said that some vampires take a while for it to set in, like delayed shock or something. Could it be that? She had a pretty traumatic event just before turning."

Abby tilted her head, considering. "It's possible," she consented. "It doesn't feel that way to me, but I could be wrong. I'm still just getting to know her, but I thought I'd give you a heads-up. Keep an eye on her. I don't think she's dangerous or anything, but she might need a little help sometimes."

Just then, Cassandra walked up. "Everything all right?"

"Of course," I replied. "I was just getting to know the world's oldest vampire."

"We were having such a lovely conversation, and you had to ruin it," she muttered, turning and walking away.

I chuckled and turned back to Cassandra. "Everything okay with Shayna?"

She nodded. "She's just trying to make sure nothing like that happens again. She seems kind of upset it happened at all, on her watch. Shayna takes her job very, very seriously."

At that, I kind of (only kind of) started to feel bad about jumping down her throat before. Not bad enough to apologize, but kind of bad.

Cassandra led me out of the office and upstairs. The Coven House was really quite massive. She brought me into a bedroom, which my male mind couldn't help but take notice of, before quickly shoving it aside. "I just thought some quiet would be nice," she explained without my asking.

We sat on the bed. "I actually kind of like it here," she went on. "It's like a family, but no one bothers you." She brushed her hair behind her ears and folded her legs on the bed. "I mean, everyone kind of keeps their distance and does their own thing, but it's like a little community too."

"It sounds nice," I said, and it actually did. I was surprised to hear myself say it, but I meant it.

Without warning, she leaned in and kissed me. It was a light kiss, but not like one you'd give a sibling. She lingered a moment and then pulled back, smiling shyly. "You should come and stay here too. It's got to be better than your lonely apartment, and despite what happened tonight, it is safer. There are guardians for during the day."

If I still breathed, I would have been breathless. I nodded dumbly instead. "I think I may just do that." Though I kind of felt she could have convinced me to do anything at that point, because she leaned into me and rested her head on my shoulder. I got to do just what I'd been resisting earlier and wrapped my arms around her.

If it hadn't been for, you know, everything else that was going on, it would have been an almost perfect moment.

CHAPTER THIRTY-TWO

I stayed at the Coven House for a little while and just spent some really nice time with Cassandra. I tried not to let things get to me for a while, and it mostly worked. That was a nice change of pace.

In the midst of one of these moments, however, an idea came entirely out of left field and hit me on the head like a foul ball. I started thinking about my ex, but not in any way that Cassandra would be offended about. I started thinking about how strangely she'd been acting, and I wondered if there was something more going on. I decided to talk to her.

It turned out to be easier to make the decision than to carry it out, but that was usually the way of life.

Although I didn't want to leave Cassandra, I didn't want her with me for this conversation. I made my farewells, making her promise to be careful and stay safe, and the way she smiled at me nearly made me lose my resolve to leave altogether, but I kept going.

I called Raven's cell, but there was no answer. She didn't have a home phone. I sent her a text message, but I didn't get a response to that either. I went to her house, where she lived in an apartment above the detached garage, but no one answered when I knocked on the door.

My initial avenues of inquiry faded fast.

So, I decided to do that which I really didn't want to do.

I had to go back to Phoenix.

☾○☽

Though I'm not a literary master, I can say that I realized my return to a club called Phoenix was appropriate. I was rising from the dead, so to speak.

I walked in and found everyone exactly as I had left them, with the exception of Raven and I. Otherwise, it was like none of them had moved or changed in the two weeks since I had walked out and then sent text messages to tell them I wouldn't be around anymore. I saw surprise in their faces, although less surprise than I would have expected.

Then again, maybe it was just arrogance to think I had that much impact on their lives one way or the other. The liquor probably would have been missed more than I had been.

No, it *definitely* would have been.

"Thought you weren't coming around anymore," Tony commented casually.

"I'm looking for Raven." There was no sense in bullshitting, I figured. That gnawing in the back of my head, the void, had come back screaming the moment I walked through the door. It got worse when I realized just how little had changed here while so much had changed for me. "I thought she might be here. Can't get her on her phone."

Geoffrey smothered a giggle in his glass. "We heard you dumped her on her ass when she tried to jump you. Twice." Even the glitter was exactly the same. Maybe he just never took a shower. There was so much gel in his hair, who could tell the difference?

I shrugged. I didn't exactly feel good about it, but I didn't feel bad either and if she was involved in any of this, I wasn't going to feel bad at all. "I guess I did. I won't lie. But I need to ask her something. I need to find her. It's really important.

Can any of you point me in the right direction?"

Tony shrugged, which shook one of the girls on his shoulders. She was either high or passed out. I couldn't tell. "She doesn't leave us with an itinerary. She might be around later, or she might not." He looked at Geoffrey, who returned the look in a moment of silent communication I could see but not interpret.

"She's been badmouthing you pretty hard lately," the glittery one finally admitted. "It's just a lot of shit. She's probably just pissed that you turned her down, knowing her hard-on for vampires, which she told us had happened to you. Hell, aside from that, I can't even remember what she's been saying, other than it's stupid for her to go off on not getting back with you when she's already been hanging all over someone else."

"If you ask me, she did better with you," Tony commented, taking a swig of his drink. "I mean, this guy is little and scrawny. And kind of funny-looking…goofy-looking."

That word caught my attention and jumped up and down on my suspicion, making me forget what I normally would've thought about how any of them would be able to tell if someone looked strange. Geoffrey went and finished it off. "He's not cute at all and looks like he hasn't eaten in months. Just looks like most of his skin sunk in on his bones. And his eyes are really kind of weird. Set really far apart on his head, like some kind of animal."

I figured we had a winner here. "If you see her, tell her I'm looking for her," I said and then in a moment of uncharacteristic politeness, I added, "Thanks."

"Don't mention it," Geoffrey replied.

They all went back to doing what they had been doing.

☾O☽

After I left Phoenix, I went to the office. I had another epiphany. I was already running all over Hell and creation, so I might as well add to the list.

Walking in, I greeted Madison. Then I asked, "Is Dakota in tonight?" She shook her head. "Can you give me her cell number?"

Once I had it, I went back outside and called her. She picked up after a couple of rings, and I got over the initial "it's me" part pretty fast before diving into business. "I was wondering if you could track someone down for me."

If she was surprised, I didn't hear it in her voice. "Who?"

"An ex of mine named Raven. Well, her real name is Henrietta Loenstein, but she goes by Raven."

Dakota snorted. "Let me guess. Black hair, too much eye make-up, black clothes always worn too tight, fishnets, and black platforms? Thought she was an outcast before, but is trendy now that there really are vampires in the world?"

"Pretty much."

"I thought you'd have better taste than that, D."

I tried not to roll my eyes. I needed her help, not a lecture, but as I did need the former, I couldn't really argue my point or my wounded pride. "Well, let's say my taste has improved since I joined the bloodsucking crowd, okay? Can you help me or not?"

Her long silence made it clear she could do without my impatience. "I'm going out of state tomorrow morning, early flight, but I'll see what I can turn up for you this evening."

"Thank you, Dakota."

"Right." She hung up.

She was doing me a favor, so I wasn't going to worry about her manners. Besides, it's not like I had any room to talk. I was just grateful for the help. I needed to find Raven, so I could call her an idiot and tell her what sort of fucker she'd fallen in with.

After that, I realized I didn't really have anything left to do but dwell on my futile frustration. So, I went back to the Coven House and just completed my circuit.

CHAPTER THIRTY-THREE

I felt better as I sat in the Coven House kitchen with Cassandra. We were sharing a glass of blood while I waited on Dakota's call, because I didn't have anything else to do. My anger subsided a little, at least down to a dull roar, while I talked with her, even if the topic didn't get us too far away.

"Why do you think Raven's involved?" she asked across the butcher block counter.

"I can't say exactly." I absently twirled the glass in my hand. "It's just a feeling, because we may not have been the loves of each other's lives, but I did know her, and the last two times I've seen her, something hasn't been right. True, she thought vampire legality was the best thing ever, but still. It's still me. I don't think the fangs would change that, even for her. She was trying to get to me, and—" I paused, wondering if I should say this next part.

She tilted her head, her expression curious, but she waited patiently.

I sighed. "I'm suspicious that maybe your slip on the floor wasn't an accident, but that Raven showed up and you two had a scuffle."

"Why do you think that?" Cassandra's expression still said everything. It was like reading a book. She didn't like the idea, but it wasn't disbelief.

"Again, a feeling, but she had a bandage on her neck, right where a vampire might bite. If she showed up and got pushy with you, you'd react like a vampire does. You'd fight back and bite her."

Her nose wrinkled. "I suppose it's possible, and maybe I hit my head after that and that's why I don't remember, but I hope not. I don't like that idea."

Well, I couldn't say I liked it either, but it felt a lot more likely than Cassandra just slipping. It made sense to me.

After we finished eating, we spent a little more time hanging out and being with one another. The Coven House was surprisingly normal. It had satellite, high-def TV, blu-ray, and several video game consoles. Vampires were up on technology. I approved of that.

I learned that one of them even had their own WoW Guild, but it wasn't on my server. Still, fangs were way geekier than I thought.

While we sat on the couch and watched one of the other vampires—I didn't catch his name—play one of the many music-themed console games, my phone rang. I recognized Dakota's number and excused myself to answer it.

"Your girlfriend was incredibly easy to track." She wasn't much for preamble.

"Ex-girlfriend." It felt important to correct that.

"Whatever. She was ridiculously easy to find. She walked from her place. I got the scent and tracked her to some dive a few streets down. She's still there. I'm heading off, but I don't see any evidence she plans to leave soon." She gave me the address and hung up.

"Thanks," I said into the dead phone.

Well, that was...ridiculously easy. I said good-bye to Cassandra, telling her where I was headed, and then went to the address Dakota gave me.

When I got there, I didn't see Dakota anywhere and figured she'd left like she said she would, though from what I knew of her abilities, it really didn't matter. She could be anyone, anywhere.

The building was an old house converted to a multi-family home. The lights were on in the downstairs apartment, which was the one Dakota had directed me to. I sat in my car and tried to figure out how best to make the approach, when the decision was made for me. Raven walked out, alone, and started down the street.

Slipping out of my car, I hurried with a little vampire speed and caught up to her. I grabbed her arm and hauled her into the space between houses, pushing her back against the wall. The anger that had grown quiet now returned with a vengeance.

She squeaked as she hit the wall but then stared open-mouthed at me.

"You," I growled, "have made a very bad choice of friends lately."

"It's not my fault," she said quietly. I heard her swallow. "He's... He..."

I arched a brow, waiting. "He *what*?"

Seeing I wasn't about to rip her throat out, yet, she wrapped her arms around herself and hunched back. "He's got crazy power over people. I mean, I thought he was kind of creepy at first, but he can just make you feel all these things. I didn't like trying to get to you. I was done with you." She managed to find a sneer for me. "But he really wanted me to, and he can be really persuasive."

"Why does he want to get at me?" I knew he did, though I still didn't understand *why*.

"Some chick named Cielle. I guess she turned him and left him. He hates her and 'cause of her, he hates you and that girl you turned."

I ran my hand through my hair. Shit, he was after Cassandra too? So, he hadn't broken into the Coven House for me. Damn it. At least security was increased now. "And you were okay with helping him try to kill me and Cassandra? I mean, you've had your fucked-up moments, Raven, but this seems low even for you."

She frowned. "He never said he wanted to *kill* you," she retorted, but I could see the gears turning in her eyes. If he hated me that much, what else did he plan to do? "I thought he just wanted to fuck with you a little, get a little revenge." Her tone was less certain now, though. "I really didn't think he wanted to kill you, D. Why do you think that?"

I looked at her like she was the stupidest person in the world, because at that moment, I was pretty sure he was. "He killed Cielle, Rave. And he attacked me outside my job, and he definitely looked like a man who wanted to kill me."

"I didn't know." She bit her bottom lip. I used to think it was cute. "I'm sorry, D. You gotta believe me, I didn't know."

"It doesn't matter." I felt my fangs poking into my bottom gums and lisped my words. I think she noticed, because she shrank in on herself. "What's his name?" I'm not sure why I cared, but I did.

She swallowed hard again. "Xavier."

"Where is he?"

"I don't know," she said, shifting uncomfortably. I stared at her for a long moment. "I really don't!"

"I'd make a break for it while you have the chance," I told her in a surprising moment of altruism, "because you never know when he'll decide he doesn't need you anymore."

More uncertainty and fear flooded her eyes. She nodded shakily and then slipped away from me. I let her go. But she stopped and turned back. "He's got someone else working with him," she told me. "I don't know his name, or much about him, but he's around sometimes and was with me that second time I saw you. Xavier told him to go with me, but he didn't tell me why. He's really skittish and doesn't like confrontation. I don't know if he's someone you need to worry about, but..." She didn't seem to know how to finish that statement, because she walked away.

Without more to go on and not being a cop or masked avenger or something, I couldn't do anything more right away, so I did my best impression of a ping pong ball and bounced back to the Coven House. I had to get Cassandra out of there.

CHAPTER THIRTY-FOUR

It wasn't until I was driving away that I realized just how angry I was. Who was I really angry at? That was the question. Raven, Xavier, Cielle, myself...or maybe all of us combined. Seeing the death grip I had on the steering wheel, I figured I had enough rage for everyone. Maybe Cielle the most, because she started it, but that didn't feel right because she was dead and all, so she'd paid for her sins.

If she was wandering around as a ghost, she was still paying. The problem was that the rest of us were paying along with her.

Cassandra was still in the living room when I got there. The guitar hero was gone, and she was reading. Hearing me enter, she looked up. "Did you find anything out? Did she attack me?"

I stopped in my tracks. *You are such an idiot, D.* "You know, I didn't even get to that. I asked her about the ass she's been running around with. But right now, I need Quintus. C'mon, we're heading to Five." While she gathered her stuff and we headed to the car, I told her what I *did* learn.

"What do you think we should do?" she asked from the passenger seat as we made our way down the drive of the Coven House.

"I don't know." I scrubbed my hand through my hair and sighed. "Now that I've gone after Raven, he'll know I'm on to him. I doubt he'll be easy to find, and I don't know if I want to go after him. He's a murderer. It doesn't sound like a smart idea. I'd call the cops, but I have no evidence, and Quintus said there wasn't anything at the time. And if he's really gunning for us, I don't know I want to stick around and wait for him."

Cassandra nodded thoughtfully. "We could've stayed at the Coven House. Despite that one event, I still believe it's secure."

I shrugged. "I suppose, but do we want to hide forever?" I slouched back into the seat, driving almost by autopilot. "We could move, I suppose." It was amazing how easy that 'we' fell in there. "I know the South. Not that I'd want to move near my family, I doubt they'd handle my new condition that well, but I know the area." Sighing, I shook my head. "I'm building a life here, though. I don't know I want to leave it."

"I don't think I'd want to move either. I've lived here for my entire life. Besides, if we run, won't we just have to keep running?"

"That's true," I agreed.

She reached out and put her hand over mine on the shifter. "Come on, it's getting late. Dawn will come soon, which will stop all of us, including this Xavier. Tomorrow night, we'll figure out what to do." She paused. "Maybe you should call the cops anyway and let them know what you know. Even if they have no evidence, it would be something."

"Five first." We were almost there, and when I had my mind set on something, I damn well wouldn't let it go.

Not that I got a lot of time to think about it.

I looked in my rear view and saw headlights getting dangerously big as the car behind me, which seemed to have just appeared, came up too fucking close. I frowned and wondered who the asshole was.

Before I could even give voice to it, I felt some freakishly overwhelming fatigue slam into me and drive me down into the steering wheel. The last thing I heard was Cassandra shouting, wheels screeching, and glass breaking.

(○)

I was dreaming.

This was very odd. I knew I was dreaming, and I knew I didn't dream anymore. It also wasn't like those dream-like moments I'd had recently. It wasn't even like any dream I'd had as a human, but I knew very strongly that it wasn't reality.

Everything was white. It was like something from a movie with fuzzy edges.

Cielle sat on a white couch in front of me.

"You're a shit, D. You know that, right?" she asked without looking at me. I couldn't tell what she was looking at, but it was something apparently in the distance.

"In my defense, I do actually know that." I walked to the couch and sat. "What the hell is going on here? Am I in the Matrix?"

She smiled, apparently unable to help herself, and now looked at me. "You're dreaming, and it's the only way I can reach you right now. Believe me, I've been trying, but I can't make you dream. I can only use the sleep someone else puts on you." She paused. "Cassandra is unique. She is a remarkably open individual, but conflicted. Her mind is complex and difficult to navigate. It wasn't easy to try to reach you from there either."

I shook my head. "You've been trying to possess her, haven't you?" That piece clicked into place. I should have figured it out sooner. "You really just do like to use people, don't you?"

The smile faded. "This is important, D, so keep your bitterness to yourself. Is the life I gave you really that bad?" She held up a hand. "Don't answer that. We don't have time." Cielle inhaled slowly. "Sunset has come and gone, but you're buried under the remains of your car and being kept asleep by the lingering power of a necromancer. I don't know how Xavier did it, but he's gotten one to help him. Xavier will have no power over you, but a necromancer will."

My mind went back to the person Raven talked about. Maybe I should have paid more attention. "Why is that..." I trailed off, and ice filled me. "What's happening outside?" I stood abruptly.

"Xavier's necro found you. Got you parked the hard way. Xavier's intent on killing you. I don't know how she did it, I couldn't see it all, but somehow, Cass convinced him to take her instead and let you live."

"What the hell did she do that for?" My mind raced. What the fuck was she thinking?

Cielle shook her head. "She loves you, D. For some reason, she does. Even as quickly as it's happened, she does... like it was meant to be...and she's sacrificing herself to save you. Xavier is torn up. I can't believe she wasn't kept asleep by the necromancer's power like you were. I don't know how she convinced him, but she did. I don't know what he's going to do to her, though. He's confused and in a lot of pain."

"Pain that you caused him," I snapped.

She winced, looking away. "Yes, this is my fault, but we don't have time to punish me, all right? I think I'm being punished enough." Opening her eyes, she turned her gaze on me again. "You can still save her, but you have to do it now. He's chosen the two of you because he's already killed me, and he needs to vent his rage. I don't think you have much time, so you need to wake the fuck up, D, and go rescue her. D? *Wake up!*"

CHAPTER THIRTY-FIVE

Cielle's final scream still echoed in my head as it drove me out of the magically induced sleep. My eyes fluttered open, and I was uniquely aware of the flashing lights and the unnatural bend of my neck. The sound of heavy handheld machinery reverberated off the inside of my eardrums. Alongside it, Cielle's words burned in the forefront of my skull.

"He's conscious!" somebody called out over the noise.

Gigantic hands, nearly the size of skillets, got a grip under my arms and pulled me awkwardly out of twisted metal.

"Be careful of his spine!" The first voice said this.

"It doesn't matter. He's a vampire. He'll heal." That rumbling I recognized as Quintus and was grateful to see his rough, dark face when my eyes were free of my metal prison. I didn't think too much about why or how he was there, though I was dimly aware of being within sight of 5. Maybe he'd seen the lights.

"What the hell happened?" I croaked, but Cielle's words answered. "Wait... Fuckin' necromancer."

Panic flooded me, and I scrambled to my feet as my vampiric healing caught my body up to itself, although Quintus was trying to hold me back. "What do you mean?" he asked.

I gave him the shortened version while firefighters

were packing in their gear, since there was no one else to rescue. I knew Cassandra was gone, and I had to go get her. She was in the hands of that fucking freak. "Quintus, I need a car," I said, grabbing his shoulders. "I have to get her."

He stared into my eyes for a long moment, like he was trying to decide whether I had a concussion. When he had decided I wasn't delusional, he gave me his keys and held up one automotive.

"Cielle's," he said simply. "She *did* want you to have it."

I sprinted the short distance to the bar and found her car without trouble, throwing myself behind the driver's seat. In any other moment, I would have taken the time to really enjoy it.

But right then, I didn't have the fucking time. *I had to do something.* The engine came to life under my hands. It and I together felt more alive than I ever had when my heart had been beating. It thrummed with eagerness to do something. I jammed the clutch and shifted, gunning it out of that parking lot, and Hell followed with me.

What exactly did I think I was going to do? As I sped through the night, I knew that I had no fucking idea. I might have been born to grow into broad shoulders and now had enhanced vampire strength, and that was enough to scare off obnoxious bigots in a graveyard, but what did I think I was going to do against a necromancer? The words of wisdom from both Sarah and Madison still rang clear in my head. I was an IT guy. I'd spent most of my life behind a computer screen. I wasn't cut out for stuff like this.

But Cielle had chosen me for a reason. I knew that now. Maybe if I hadn't been such an ass and bailed on her like I did, I might have been able to help her. I couldn't ever know for sure, but I felt certain of it in my heart. I had been thinking about it a lot since I learned she was dead, after all, and this was my final conclusion.

One thing, of course, was clearest. I wasn't going to let

anything happen to Cassandra.

My head pounded, but I ignored it. I couldn't get over the idea that she had sacrificed herself for me. She knew he might kill her, so why? How had she not been overtaken by the necromancer? Was she nuts? I just couldn't get my brain around it. If I wasn't in time and something happened to her, because of me... I'd never be able to live with myself. I couldn't be late.

I wasn't going to be late.

Screeching to a halt in front of the house I'd caught Raven at earlier, as it was my best guess to find them, I jammed the car in park and blazed out of it. I still didn't have a plan other than get inside and crack some skulls. It was what every instinct inside was telling me to do and since my brain didn't have a better plan, we were all just going along with it.

Getting to the door, I grabbed the handle and found it was locked. I tore it off the hinges and stormed into the room. There across from me was a second scrawny little guy, there seemed to be a profusion of them these days, sitting with a piece of fabric open on the floor before him. I had no clue what he was doing, and I didn't really care. He was staring at the door, though, obviously having heard me tear it off.

"Stop," he said without conviction, getting to his feet. He held his hands, and I felt the tingle. I knew that magic was at work and if I hadn't known this guy was The Necromancer before, I knew it now.

It's hard to accurately describe what it felt like. It was like when you feel a strong urge to do something you know you shouldn't, like go out of the house at ten at night to buy a pint of ice cream when you don't have a pregnant wife. I felt this deep-in-the-brain compulsion to turn around and leave, but I knew I shouldn't. I couldn't let myself give into the compulsion, no matter how strong or how it sunk from my mind into my muscles.

Every step was a struggle, like moving through syrup, but I managed to inch my feet forward.

Necromancer's eyes were wide, shocked. I guessed he'd never had this happen before, or maybe he looked like that all the time. I didn't know. I didn't care. I knew Cassandra was on the other side of him, I just *knew*, and I had to get there, no matter what magic-casting asshole was in my way.

He began chanting quietly. I couldn't understand what he was saying or even hear it clearly enough to know what it was in the first place. I felt ants starting to crawl all over my skin, but without the ants. Fire ants, burning paths everywhere their invisible little feet tread. It hurt like hell in a way I'd never known, and I screamed. I admit it. It hurt.

The pain stopped me in my tracks for a moment. I squeezed my eyes shut and could feel the syrup thicken around my body. His magic was intensifying, and it pushed against every piece of me.

I had to remember why I was here. This was just the bastard using his magic. If I could get past this and get to him, I could make it stop. If I could make it stop, I could get through this room to the other side and find Cassandra. She was being held by a bastard who was going to hurt her. I had to get there. I had to not waste time getting tripped up by this necromancer.

Repeating what I had to do and why I had to do it helped me to start ignoring the pain. It still hurt. I couldn't make it go away without getting across the room, but it helped me to ignore it. I opened my eyes and began inching my way forward again.

The chanting stopped, and his mouth dropped open. I felt a shift in the powers working on my psyche. It was still syrup and it still hurt, but I felt a very specific compulsion now to turn around. The thick air behind me cleared. There was less pain behind me. If I turned around and left, it would all stop. It would all be okay.

No, damn it, I couldn't turn around. I had to move forward. I dragged each foot forward, and every step was an inch closer to the source of my agony. My feet and legs burned with the struggle, but I could see panic in magic man's eyes. He was freaking out and just wanted me to leave. He was afraid of me. Knowing he was afraid gave me power and when I realized I had power, cracks began to creep through the compulsions. Slowly, they began to lose their hold.

He felt it, too. Aside from afraid, he just looked bewildered. "How are you doing that?"

His question made the cracks open a little further. I began to move a little faster and was almost across the room. He was nearly in arm's reach, but he realized this and put out one more blast of power. The magic drove nails into my feet and froze me where I was as he backed into the doorway. His back thudded dully while he pressed into me, metaphysically speaking.

I was weakening. I could feel it. The strain of pressing against this much magic was wearing me down. Even vampires don't have infinite stamina, but I just had to remind myself of why I was here.

Cassandra. That drive, that hunger, in the back of my mind screamed louder than ever, but it screamed for her. It screamed for me to not let another person down. It screamed that this was important. I couldn't turn my back on it. I couldn't run away from it. I couldn't let myself do what I'd done my whole life.

I had to do something.

Roaring, I yanked my arms forward and powered through the last shreds of the necromancer's magic. He gasped, and the power shattered. I stumbled forward when it released its hold but regained my balance quickly. I gasped as well, relieved to escape the pain, but then surged ahead and grabbed the necromancer by the front of his shirt as he gaped and squawked. I thought he tried to say something, but I didn't know what it was.

"Leave. Now," I said through gritted teeth, lifting him off his feet.

He scrabbled at my hands. "I will!" he squeaked.

I half-tossed him behind me and watched just long enough to see him rush out the front. Meanwhile, I turned back to the inner door.

I gained the second room, feeling like I'd just leveled in some video game.

In the next room, I found Xavier, Cassandra, and a fuckload of sharp implements.

Chapter Thirty-Six

I knew there was no chance of a surprise entry, so I burst through the door without care for subtlety.

Once inside, I found the two of them, but thankfully no one else. Cassandra knelt on the floor, and Xavier stood over her, pointing a fucking sword at her, of all things. It wasn't the most expert hold ever. After I got past the initial gut-wrench at the scene itself, I tried to calculate if I could get to him before he took her head off. It was easy enough to decide I couldn't afford to take the chance.

"You shouldn't have come," Cassandra said with a smile both grateful and sad.

"What are you doing, Xavier?" I asked, focusing on him. I didn't know what I was going to do now, but I had to do something.

He seemed startled, at first, when I used his name, but he got over it quickly enough. "I'm doing what I have to do." It sounded like a line from a badly written movie, but I wasn't going to point that out. "Cielle was evil, and I have to stamp out everything she left behind."

I didn't like the sound of that. "Wouldn't that include you?"

"It will," he said, too easily. "When I'm done with the two of you."

This still didn't make sense. Why had he let Cassandra talk him into taking just her, if he meant to kill me anyways?

Did he just want to lure me out, perhaps thinking he'd get caught in the Coven House?

"Cielle was kind of fucked up, but that doesn't mean there's anything wrong with Cassandra or me. She did you wrong, but that doesn't mean you have to take it out on us," I argued, knowing I would never be on the psychiatric team called in for ledge-walkers.

"Shut up," he snapped, swinging the sword in my direction.

The place was a museum of old weapons. Glancing around, I saw a battered round shield leaning against the wall nearby. What the hell? If he was going to point sharp things at me, I was going to damn well armor up. With vampire quickness, I snatched it up and held it like some Spartan badass. At least I felt that way at that point.

Now that he was focused on me, though, I had more options. I didn't care if I got cut, but I couldn't let Cassandra get hurt. So, I took a chance and ran at him.

At my charge, Xavier did the same. Despite what had looked like an inexpert grip, he showed some skill as he swung in swift repetition. I had to throw the shield up again and again to stave off his attacks, but after several strikes and the feeling of being pushed back, the rage and hunger erupted again within me. Whatever fatigue had come vanished in the face of this challenge and this adversary.

Roaring with a volume that only vampires can attain, I used my size and sheer will power to begin to push back, rather than just defend. I caught him off guard and claimed some territory.

He reclaimed his nerve after only a minute and swung down at me with an overhand strike that I caught off the shield. A hard clang echoed through the room, and it reverberated through me, reminding me of the efforts I had already made this night. I would not fucking give in to this little shit, however, so I hung on.

It was repetitive. Hit and block. Hit and block. The hits came from different sides, but I swung that board around fast enough to catch them, though some just barely. His rage matched my own, and this fight was only going to be won by the one of us that *wanted* it the most. I hate to admit it, but I began to feel it all bearing me down.

One such moment found me not swinging around fast enough and getting a small slice to my shoulder. It was a minor wound, but enough to hurt like hell. I shouted something incoherent and charged him again, back to the hit and block.

Suddenly, I saw an opening and grabbed it with preternatural swiftness. I smacked my shield into his sword, pinning it to the wall. I would have had him had the bastard not used his free hand to grab a silver stiletto from places unknown and jam it into the easiest place he could reach, which happened to be my side. Vampires being just as allergic to silver as every supernatural, the poison coursed through me.

I screamed. Maybe there were actual words, but I doubted it. Before the silver bore me down, I surged forward and caught him entirely unprepared. He had expected me to fall, but I damn well wasn't going to give him the pleasure. With his bag of tricks empty, I swung the shield and hit him across the face. He fell to the ground. I followed him down and hit him again. The fury demanded I beat him until he was unrecognizable. My free hand had even gripped his hair, rage bleeding off me as I slammed his skull into the hard floor, over and over, while my shield pinned his sword arm down. I craved. I could almost taste his death, and it was going to taste *good*.

I might have beaten his head flat but for a voice that found its way through my dark anger and a light hand on my shoulder.

"D, don't."

It sounded like Cassandra at first, but then it sounded like Cielle.

"D."

The voice was soft, but persistent. I stopped banging but didn't let go of Xavier as blood oozed from his wounds. He was still conscious, groaning beneath me. I trembled with the desire to finish what I'd started.

"D, let him go." The voice wrapped around me. I felt the elemental magic of it and began to resist, but it was Cassandra's hand. I felt it and gave myself over to it, letting the shield and the vampire go. I staggered to my feet. I looked at her, but the curve of her mouth and the angle of her brows made her look not like herself. She turned to Xavier, who was still in one piece enough to start sitting up, looking at her with fear.

"Xavier."

Hearing her voice, he shrieked and tried to crab-walk away, but he only fell back again. "What the fuck?!"

"It's me, Xavier."

"It can't be." His expression was bloody and horrorstricken. "I killed you. I cut your fucking head off."

"Yes, you did, but Cassandra was kind enough to let me speak with you." She smiled sadly. "Xavier, I'm sorry."

The horror faded into confusion. "What?"

She shook her head and sighed. "I'm sorry. I never meant to hurt you. I tried to tell you when you found me that night, but you wouldn't listen. I'm sure that's my fault, too. I don't blame you. I abandoned you."

"This doesn't sound like you, Cielle," he said, still clearly wrestling with his disbelief. So was I. I was also wrestling with a harsh anger that wanted to grab him and keep at it, but I stopped myself from doing so. The poison weakening me helped that, too.

"Wandering around in non-corporeal form tends to

give you a lot of time for self-reflection," she said. "It's me, Xavier. You were turned toward the end of World War Two. You were dying of a battle injury, and I saved your life. At that time, you said you were excited by the prospect of a new life."

The disbelief was gone. "You were like my family, Cielle. Why did you leave me?" he whispered. "Why did you abandon me?"

Cassandra/Cielle shook her head. "I was just being selfish. I have no excuse, so I won't try to make any. I will say it again. I'm sorry. I wish that I could change it now, but I can't. But don't make D and Cassandra pay for what I did wrong. It's a sin, Xavier. It's not redemption or saving anyone's souls. It's just murder. Don't make it worse than it is."

His face crumbled, and he began sniffing like he was crying, though vampires lacked tears so it was dry, but he was crying. Cassandra/Cielle moved toward him and folded him into her arms.

Weakly, from my silver-poisoned self, I watched. I had no part in this, other than as a witness. I felt like an intruder, now that I was a little calmer. Xavier buried himself against her like a little kid, and I felt the tingle on my skin. Magic, but this time, I knew it was Cassandra's.

Could she heal a broken mind? I supposed she could.

We all sat like that for a long time. I wanted to say something, but I knew that I shouldn't. There was something happening here that was...bigger than me. Unfortunately, there was no magic to reconcile all the images: Cielle as a selfish succubus but also as redeemed ghost, Xavier as cold-blooded killer but also wounded child, Cassandra as an innocent vampire and extraordinary healer, and me as... I didn't even know what I was anymore, but I knew it was quiet in my mind.

Finally, Xavier pulled away from Cassandra. He looked warily between the two of us. "Are you still..." he began but hesitated.

"It's Cassandra," she said with a smile that showed how okay she had apparently been with being possessed. She reached out and touched his cheek in an almost motherly gesture, which both fit and didn't.

"I'm sorry," he whispered. He looked at me and repeated his apology. "I've just been so torn apart since Cielle left me. It... It wasn't romantic. I'm not, like, a jilted lover or something." He paused and covered his face. "Not that that could make it better or worse, but she was like family. I had none and then I had her. She became my world and when she just left, no word and no message, I lost it. I had to find her, but she started running from me, and I just got more and more hurt and..." He sighed, shoulders slumping. "I'm sorry."

"It'll be all right now," Cassandra said with assurance.

"What do we do now?" I asked. "I kind of...might need help?"

Her pale eyes blinked. "D!" she exclaimed, just remembering (apparently) that I'd been hurt. She rushed to my side, and I felt warmth flooding me. My shoulder knit, and the weakness faded.

"Thank you," I said quietly.

She kissed me on the forehead.

CHAPTER THIRTY-SEVEN

What is considered a normal life for a vampire, IT guy, animator bouncer, and healer bodyguard? I still don't know, even now.

We left the house that night, and Xavier turned himself into the police for killing Cielle and kidnapping Cassandra. They said there might be mitigating circumstances for the psychological aspect, but he'd still be spending some time in jail. It didn't look like the idea bothered him. Maybe it was self-imposed penance. I didn't ask. Personally, I didn't really want to see him again. I felt bad for him getting dumped by Cielle, but I didn't want anything to do with him.

The necromancer was lost to the wind, never to be seen again.

Cielle didn't visit us through Cassandra again. I thought I saw a glimpse of her in a daydream, smiling and fading away. Maybe vampire ghosts were like human ghosts, after all. They just needed to solve whatever was holding them in place.

After taking some time to recuperate, Cassandra and I joined the coven. I had expected a big ceremony, but it turned out we just needed Jade's approval. We moved in the next day. I switched servers and joined *Fangs for the Memories*, the coven's guild. It seemed only right.

I decided to talk to Sadie at some point to see if I could expand on my role at the office, although I had no idea into what. Cassandra wondered if she could offer her healer's services, but I worried that might end up taxing her too much. It was tabled for later discussion.

There were a lot of things being held over for later discussions. There was a lot about Cassandra I still needed to know, and a lot of questions, but it was all for later. I was just going to celebrate life, or whatever it was we had, for the now of it all.

Returning home from a job one night, maybe a week after everything, I found Cassandra and Abby sitting on the living room floor together. There was a deck of cards between them, but they weren't playing poker. I recognized them as some kind of Tarot deck.

"I didn't know you could read those," I commented, sitting on the couch.

"I'm just full of surprises," Abby said.

I snorted. "Can't argue with that."

Her eyes flickered up with a dry look before turning back to the cards.

"She's going to teach me," Cassandra said with a smile.

"I imagine it will take a while," I said this to Abby.

She stopped her hand before turning over the last card. Obviously, she could tell my words were directed at her. Without reply, she flipped the last one over. The Sun.

Even I could figure that one out, sort of.

"I've got the time," she said.

A little while later, Cassandra and I headed outside for a walk. Summer was in full bloom and even midnight was warm and a little sticky, but I didn't mind. Vampires, kind of like lizards, like the heat. I suppose it reminds us of the sun we can no longer go out in.

"Is there anything you can do to help her?" I asked quietly. I still thought she was a creepy little shit, but she was helping Cassandra, so she couldn't be all bad.

"No." She shook her head. "It's up to her, but I think maybe it will be okay."

I was coming to learn that she usually seemed to be right about these things, so I didn't argue. I figured she'd know better than I did.

"And you?" she asked me after a moment, glancing sidelong at me. "How are you doing with things? There's been a lot of change lately."

"There certainly has." I chuckled, stuffing my hands into my pockets. "But I'm okay. I'm glad things have turned out okay, or as okay as they can be. I'm still sorry Cielle is dead, and I doubt I'll ever stop feeling bad about that."

She touched my arm. "It's only natural, but she forgave you, though she knew there wasn't a lot to forgive in the end. She made mistakes, but she's at peace now."

"I thought she hadn't tried to touch your mind since everything with Xavier?" I asked, briefly concerned.

Cassandra shook her head. "She hasn't. It's what I picked up that night and also can just figure out on my own."

I nodded. "I see." It was good to know, although after the dream—or whatever it had been—that I'd had, I kind of already knew.

As we walked, we passed one of the Coven House wardens who was also taking a walk around the grounds, although his had purpose. He nodded at us and we nodded back, both going our ways. It was quiet and easy. Things were back to normal, or at least as normal as they would ever be, I supposed.

We found a place to sit in the grass, and I let the quiet fill me. There weren't a lot of woodland animals in this forest, being near the bloodsuckers and all, and the only cars were far off. It was peaceful here. I kind of let myself take root for a while, because tonight, and for days now, the voracious drums had been silent. I had the feeling they wouldn't be coming back.

Author's Note

This one was a fun one. I didn't write it entirely on my own, but since my co-author was my husband, he said I could have all the credit! He's a nice fella that way.

So, this story concept and the main character was originally the creation of my husband's sixteen-year-old self and the song "Hey, Pretty" by Poe. Later, I found what he'd started and liked the idea. I wanted to finish it and add it to the Adelheid world, which he was totally cool with. Of course, the original form had all the angst that one can expect from a sixteen-year-old writing vampire fiction. I toned it down a little and just let D be angsty.

I wrote it, he reviewed and approved, and I published. Here we are!

There are little bits of my husband in D and me in Cassandra, of course, because... I mean... Why wouldn't I put that in there? This isn't the end of their story either, and I hope that you'll keep on reading the series and find out what's next.

Happy Reading!

If you want to know more about the town of Adelheid, the people who live in it, and the lore I chose to use when writing these preternatural species, you can check out my series wiki at wiki.authorkbthorne.com

Sincerely,
K. B. Thorne, September 2020

About the Author

Born a Connecticut Yankee in nobody's court, K. B. Thorne grew up to brave snow and talk fast.

She started reading when she was three and never looked back, soon frequently falling asleep with a book under her cheek. At eleven, she discovered *Night Mare* by Piers Anthony and entered the world of grown-up fantasy fiction. As you can guess, it was all over from there. She started writing at fourteen, then met vampires as a teenager and the concept for what would become Adelheid (now the Blood Rights Series) was soon born. Mia Darien followed a few years later, and the books were released.

However, K. B. is also a third-generation Trekkie. Somewhere in a vault at Paramount is a very angry letter written by her grandmother when *Star Trek: The Original Series* was cancelled, so sci-fi is in the blood too. Alongside a love of love and an adoration for her first love of epic fantasy.

K. B. Thorne is the evolution of Mia Darien after years of learning and living. She has taken both of those things to become a smarter, better writer with a fresh new face and take on the literary world. Thorne writes the urban fantasy, fantasy and sci-fi, while Sadie Johnston writes the romance.

These days, when she's not desperately trying to find time to write, she works as a freelance editor/cover artist/formatter and happily lives her unconventional life alongside her very own Named Man of the North and their mini-tank. (Who is, you know, their son.)

You can find K. B. at authorkbthorne.com

Other Books by K. B. Thorne

Writing as K. B. Thorne
Blood Rights Series

Bad Blood
Blood and Thunder
Blood Moon
Written in Blood
Bloodshot
First Blood
Out for Blood
New Blood
Flesh and Blood

Out for Blood Series
Bones & Blood

Bellator (Anthology)
Good Things (Anthology)
Ashes to Sunrise (Anthology)
The Shape of Tomorrow (Anthology)
Born of Defiance (Anthology)

Writing as Sadie Johnston (Romance)
Beauty
Help Wanted (with Viola Dawn)
Threnody (with Alastair Malone)
Here, Kitty Kitty (Anthology)
Amor Vincit Omnia (Anthology)
Second Chances (Anthology)